FUNERAL ARRANGEMENTS

"Diego!" Slocum shouted from the doorway of the shop.

The short man stopped and blinked as he pushed the sombrero up with his left hand to better see him.

"Which country would you rather die in?" Slocum asked. Diego was not to be dissuaded from his revenge. Slocum could almost predict the words he heard next.

"I have come to kill you, gringo! Where is my brother?"

"He is preparing a place for you in the next world." Perhaps Diego would reconsider—though Slocum never believed it for a moment. The die was cast, someone would die, and Slocum had no plans for his own funeral.

JAKE LOGAN

SLOCUM AND THE
REAL McCOY

JOVE BOOKS, NEW YORK

SLOCUM AND THE REAL McCOY

A Jove Book / published by arrangement with
the author

PRINTING HISTORY
Jove edition / January 1998

All rights reserved.
Copyright © 1998 by Jove Publications, Inc.
This book may not be reproduced in whole
or in part, by mimeograph or any other means,
without permission. For information address:
The Berkley Publishing Group, a member of Penguin Putnam Inc.,
200 Madison Avenue, New York, New York 10016.

The Putnam Berkley World Wide Web site address is
http://www.berkley.com

ISBN: 0-515-12208-4

A JOVE BOOK®
Jove Books are published by The Berkley Publishing Group,
a member of Penguin Putnam Inc.
200 Madison Avenue, New York, New York, 10016.
JOVE and the "J" design are trademarks belonging to
Jove Publications, Inc.

PRINTED IN THE UNITED STATES OF AMERICA

10 9 8 7 6 5 4 3 2 1

SLOCUM AND THE
REAL McCOY

1

May 10, 1880

"Come sail with me, Slocum," Captain McCulley said. The burly commander of the S.S. *Duchess Ann* stood prepared to step into the rowboat. He waited for Slocum's answer. His vessel was anchored a hundred yards away in the sparkling blue waters of the Gulf of California. The *Duchess*'s sails were already being unfurled by his crew. He would take his leave on the high tide for exciting places like Boston, New York, and Charlotte. Down the beach, screaming killdeer skirted the high tide's lap in search of food.

"McCulley, you know the sea, I know the land," Slocum said. "I think I'll stay on the land. Kinda like the firmness under my boot soles." Slocum stood with his arms folded, rocking on his boot heels. The rolling glazed blue water held no lure for him.

"Ah, but Slocum, there will be many beautiful women in my ports of call that you will miss." McCulley set his bearded face sideways as if pleading for Slocum to reconsider.

"No, I better get this merchandise up to Tucson." Slocum gave a head toss toward the array of Red River carts and wagons already loaded with the ship's cargo, goods that Don Alvares expected him to deliver in three weeks to

1

the sleepy desert town at the base of the Catalina Mountains.

"Will I see you next time?"

"A man can't tell that far in the future," Slocum said.

"I understand. My pleasure to meet a man of your intelligence in this godforsaken hole." McCulley reached to grasp his hand and shook it, then stepped into his boat and ordered the seamen to row out to the ship.

Slocum waved good-bye to him as a pair of noisy, feeding gulls ducked down and dimpled the surface of the smooth swells that lapped at his feet on the sparkling white sand. McCulley's small boat rode the easy waves as the four men worked the oars. A salty fish smell filled Slocum's nose as he watched them pull for the ship. He turned and looked at the cud-chewing teams of oxen waiting patiently under their yokes.

"Are we ready?" Tomas, his *segundo,* asked. The short, handsome youth with his sly smile sat his gray horse ready to spread word to the teamsters that it was time to go. His broad straw sombrero shaded his swarthy face from the mid-morning sun.

"Let's go to Tucson!" Slocum said aloud, and made a circle with his right hand in the air and then pointed eastward. He could see the teamsters, sitting in the shade of their rigs, struggle to their feet. No one in Sonora, Mexico, was in much of a hurry, and only Slocum's insistence that they move out would get them going.

Slocum studied the jacales and hovels called Puerto Libertad that clustered on the barren ash-white bluff above the broad beach. It was not a famous port of call, and the village was far from prospering, for few ships anchored there. The cantinas were squalid and the women who worked them were diseased castaways. He never enjoyed the layovers at this place waiting for a ship to arrive. His memory of the beauty of the Tucson's women drew a small smile to his lips before he sobered to the moment. How many of his men had contracted the clap in the four days they had been there?

In a short while, he would have to listen to the wails of those infected by the Libertad whores when they tried to pee and cried out loud in pain. Their complaints would fill the air, and the infections would be no joke. Still, he had warned them all of the dangers before they drove into the town. But he knew that a stiff prick had no caution or conscience.

He drew up the cinch and then checked it before he mounted the bay horse. With his boot toe stuck in the stirrup, he swung aboard. Wagon wheels began to cut the gritty ground, and the protest of the wooden wheels on the dry axles began to fill the air. Grateful for the heavy pointed *tapederos* that protected his toes from the many spiny plants along the road, he put his spurs to the bay and sent him loping for the front of the line.

"We are missing Manuel," Tomas reported, riding up to meet him.

"Have someone else take his wagon and drive his oxen. He can catch up when he sobers up." Slocum read the dread on the man's face. "He isn't here when we leave, then he loses his job."

"Sí, señor." Tomas turned the dish-faced gray horse and galloped off.

Slocum looked toward the village and, seeing the brown-skinned children that played around outside the buildings, he wondered what whore Manuel was on top of. The man would soon learn to take better care of his time. To be abandoned in such a place as this was surely punishment enough for him to learn his lesson. When they returned for more goods, if Manuel had not had his throat cut, he would beg for his old job back. Slocum sent the bay up the dim road in a long jog, headed for the low range of hills that rose in the east.

Maybe he would find a bighorn sheep to kill. The red hills that stretched north and south for miles along Sonora's west coast were famous for their curled-horn inhabitants. The natives called this region Terra Baldinas, a place without people or an empty land. Despite the lack of good water holes, he found many white-tailed deer and antelopes in the open country to the south of the road, and javelinas, the pig-like cactus eaters. Still, the bighorn sheep that clung to the mountains were the finest game to bag in this arid land of cactus and dry washes.

Men worked best with meat in their bellies. His cook, the snow-haired Vasquez, would remind him of this whenever he lacked game or beef to cook for the drivers.

He saw Tomas coming up from the rear. The second in command reined his gelding in beside Slocum's stirrup. Then he gave a last look at the village, shook his head, and turned back.

"No sign of him. I put the one they call Arturo in charge of his wagon."

"From now on it will be Arturo's wagon." Slocum waited for Tomas's reply.

"Manuel is a mean man and he will kill anyone who takes his wagon. He has said so before."

"Then one of us will have to kill Manuel first. These wagons and oxen are not his. They belong to the Don."

"I know, but he expects—I mean, he has always had that wagon."

"Do you fear Manuel?" He looked for the young man's reaction.

"No, señor. But I fear having to kill him."

"You have never done that?" He looked toward the mountains, which were dazzling in the heat waves.

"No, señor, never have I killed a man."

Slocum nodded as he turned back to check over his shoulder. They rode far enough ahead of the train that no one could hear their words. He turned back to his *segundo*.

"That is why I warned you about taking this job," he said.

"Ah, *sí*. I thought you meant I must kill Apaches."

"It makes no difference. There is no law out here. Neither bandits nor Apaches will ever give you a chance to think about it. They will kill you. Anyone who opposes this train must be stopped."

"I savvy, señor. If Manuel should come and cause trouble with Arturo, I will not hesitate to do as you wish."

"You will be the boss or he will be." He looked again to be certain his man understood the meaning of his words.

"I savvy, señor."

"I am going ahead and find Vasquez a fat bighorn sheep for supper." Slocum waited for Tomas's reply.

"Good luck. I will make a camp at the base of the pass."

"Good, you scout today. Sometimes a war party of Seris warriors comes ashore from their island south of here. They are very mean, swift killers. Beyond the mountains, they won't be much trouble, but they might be waiting for a fat train like ours to attack at the hills."

"I will keep my eyes open for them and for bandits."

"Good. See you at the base of the mountains." Slocum booted the bay into a long lope. Under the right fender, his well-oiled .50-caliber Spencer filled the scabbard. *Mr. Bighorn, you better watch out or Vasquez will fry your chops in his skillets tonight.* He pushed the short horse down the dim parallel tracks that bisected the dried-up desert short grass and weed stalks.

Paloverde trees with their weeping limbs dotted the chaparral. Giant saguaros that had seen the conquistadors spread their arms for balance. Clumps of tall organ-pipe cactus mixed with the rest of the spiny vegetation. Purple fruit ripened in the sprawling beds of the pancake prickly pear. Light green and bristling with needles, the cholla backed the other cactus, with their jumping joints ready to cripple a horse or ox by attaching to a fetlock.

The cholla was the reason the Mexicans never trimmed the fetlocks of their horses. A bristled section of this spiny desert plant could make a horse limp in two steps from the time it attached itself to the animal below the ankle. Only with two sticks could a rider detach the pincushion. The native ponies were shaggy-looking, but seldom were troubled with the cholla spines.

He rose in the stirrups as he looked back. His train was coming. He spotted the column of dust under the hill. No longer could he see the hovels of Libertad. He would not miss that place, nor the Mexican port official, Hector Herreras. The man was a snake with his hand out—pay him a considerable bribe or waste valuable days while he decided the tax on certain goods. Don Alvares always sent enough money to silence the man, though Slocum never paid the bribe, and always felt good afterward.

He reined up and let the bay horse blow. He removed a brass telescope from his saddlebags and tried to search the front range for sign of a sheep. Nothing moved or looked like a bighorn on the steep slopes. The sheep close to the road had obviously been thinned out by travelers. He headed south on a game trail that wound through the greasewood and cactus, watching to avoid the spiny growth that hedged the way. He had a few hours to find a good ram. Out of habit, he shifted the .44 Colt in the holster on his hip, and then gave the bay his head to cross a dry wash.

Somewhere on the mountain's face above him, a fat bighorn waited for his bullet. He checked the sun. Still plenty of time to fill his needs. He lifted the bay's head when he stumbled going up the bank, drew him up, and then when he recovered, sent him deeper into the chaparral.

A few miles on, he saw a small band of sheep rise and move up the mountain at his approach. His telescope brought in the image of a ewe and three yearlings working upward on a narrow ledge. Then he spotted the monarch in the glass.

A small whistle escaped through his teeth at the sight of the animal's horns. This one had a great three-quarter curl in each of his horns. Good enough. He would be supper tonight. Slocum let the bay pick his way through the desert to get in closer. He wanted a clear shot to drop the buck in his tracks. Many times a rider did not panic the sheep as much as a person on foot, but the male had not lived so long by being stupid. Slocum tried not to look directly at him as he closed in.

At last he drew the horse up in a thick stand of towering saguaros, and took the rifle out as he stepped down. With a shell in the chamber, he used the great girth of the cactus to hide behind as he looked through the iron V sights for the buck. Soon he found the ram sniffing the air. The range was long, but Slocum was unable to move closer. He raised the sight above the ram's heart.

The rifle's loud crack shattered the silence, and hushed the desert wrens with its echo. The ram crumpled and pitched off the steep mountain as the other sheep rushed away in panic straight up what looked like a perpendicular wall. Slocum waited with a fresh shell jacked in, but the animal landed out of sight at the base of the mountain.

The bay snorted and shied back as Slocum mounted him. His actions drew a frown from Slocum. The pony had heard gunshots before. Why had this shot upset him? Slocum had no idea. Holding the Spencer ready, he booted the bay toward the mountain. Something had the horse spooked, for Slocum had to hit him twice with his spurs, and both times the gelding made a rolling snort of distrust through his wide nostrils.

"Dammit! Get in there." Slocum's patience was wearing thin, and he spurred the pony hard enough that he finally lunged into the greasewood and headed for the mountain.

Slocum rose in the stirrups to try to see where the ram had fallen. Out of nowhere something growled as loud as a circus lion, and the bay horse shot sideways. The action threw Slocum out of his seat to the right into midair, and unable to catch the horn to save himself while holding onto the rifle, he was thrown on the ground.

The bay broke and ran away through the chaparral with his head high as Slocum rose to his knees wincing at the pain in his arm. The rifle was still in his hands as he pushed himself to his feet. He heard the snarl of a large cat as he stumbled forward, parting the creosote-smelling greasewood and seeing the ram's carcass on a pile of rocks. A large jaguar guarded it with his fangs bared, defending what he considered his own kill.

His yellow eyes flamed with anger that anyone would challenge his authority. He curled a paw of extended claws and swatted the air. Rifle butt to his shoulder, Slocum aimed for his wide mouth, and the .50's recoil socked into his shoulder in an earsplitting explosion. Gun smoke smarted his eyes as he watched the cat flip over backward from the impact of the bullet. The spotted feline thrashed on the ground in death's throes as Slocum drew his Colt and shot him again. This time the bullet stilled the animal.

Slocum dropped to his knees and studied the sleek hide with the black spots in the yellow-orange coat. The tom had been eating good and looked in the prime of life. With his thumb, Slocum peeled the tom's black lip back and studied his dental work. His teeth looked unbroken and needle sharp. His scars were few for a big male, though another cat had mauled his head once and the scars from the claw marks were like drawn lines in the hair across his scalp.

"You're a long ways from your home in the jungle, old boy," he said aloud. Damn, he had heard of these big cats but had never seen one. Helluva way to get introduced. The tom had to measure nine feet from his nose to the tip of his long tail and weigh over two hundred pounds. He'd no doubt been living off the bighorns.

Slocum winced as he rose to his feet. He had a jaguar and a sheep to skin. On top of that, he had no horse to ride to camp, and that could mean a long walk. He didn't blame the bay pony for stampeding; the gelding had smelled the big cat, and Slocum should have known something was wrong from his actions.

With an eerie feeling running up his spine, he again checked the face of the mountain. Nothing in sight. Then he bent over, drew out his skinning knife from his boot, and began the task. Maybe Tomas would discover the bay and come looking for him. Slocum cut the ram's throat, and the red blood surged out on the crumbled rocks. There were lots of things he could hope for. In the meantime, he'd better get them both skinned and dressed.

2

"You stupid sons of bitches!" Curly Bill Brocius swore out loud, and then threw his wide-brimmed felt hat on the ground. Rage forced his lower jaw to stiffen and his head tremored with a small series of earthquakes. Towering like a huge gorilla above the two short Mexican men, he let his breath rage in and out of his wide mouth. Then he began to pull on his long matted black beard to keep himself from killing both of the men on the spot. Only his extreme control saved them from meeting their Maker.

"I told you to block the road! Not lay a damn tree branch in it! Why, that idiot stage driver just ran around that like it was a dead chicken in the way!" Brocius could see the last dust of the disappearing coach as it headed north with the silver and gold still in the strongbox.

"It was all there was to put in the way," Obregon said with a shrug.

"We've planned for a week to stop that stage. Why in Christ's name didn't you get more trees?"

"Look around," Obregon said with his palms turned up. "There are no more trees."

"Nothing," the younger one called Begota added.

Brocius swept up his high-crowned hat and slapped it on his head. He searched around the treeless grassy San Bernadino Valley, which swept off to the distant purple Chiricahua range in the west and the brown Ponticellos in the east that marked New Mexico's border. There were no trees or anything to make a barricade with. Still, he had sent the two men down here to block the road so he and the others could ride out and hold up the stage when it was forced to stop.

"What we going to do now?" Stillwell Jack asked. Dressed in a canvas duster, his black mask pulled down, the gambler sat a leggy blood bay.

"Yeah, I come a long ways for this sure thing," Reno said, pulling on the ends of his silver mustache as he sat his bay pony. The shorter man was bareheaded, his flour-sack mask hung on his saddlehorn. His thin blond hair stirred in the wind, and impatiently he slapped it down and then put on his hat and jerked the chin strap tight.

"We screwed up!" Brocius said, putting his foot in the stirrup and with great effort swinging his mammoth girth into the saddle. He checked the big black horse and shook his head in disgust.

"Don't call me next time about your get-rich schemes," Stillwell Jack said. He gave Brocius and the two Mexicans a haughty look of contempt from his coal dark eyes, and then bolted away on his pacing horse.

"Same goes for me," Reno said, checking his horse. "As a dependable stage robber, you're washed up in this country, Curly Bill. Word gets out about this in Paradise, you'll be the laughingstock of every cowboy in the two territories."

"You say a damn word . . ." Brocius pointed his finger at the man.

"I won't have to tell anyone. That was Whispers Andrews up on the seat of that stage. He'll have the word out about this fiasco before you get back to the border."

Brocius waved him away. "Go join that uppity Stillwell. You deserve him. I don't need your dumb asses anyway."

"Good! Next time don't send word for me then!"

"I wouldn't piss on you if you were on fire!" Brocius shouted after Reno. Damn cowboys anyway. That was what that consumptive bastard Doc Holliday had named all of the wild bunch around Cochise County—cowboys. Made some of the Texas drovers mad, but the name stuck locally, and anyone who rode the dry gulches was called a cowboy. Besides, Doc was no man to buck, unless you wanted your own little space in that rocky hillside out on the north side of Tombstone that they called Boot Hill. The term "cowboy" meant not only the bunch that rode with the McLowerys, Old Man Clanton, or Ike, but any other independent outlaw or rustler. Kinda put them in their own fraternity whether they stayed at Paradise, Gleason, below the border at Naco, in the Huachuca Mountains, or at the old man's ranch down in Sonora. They were the cowboys.

Screw that coughing bastard Holliday and them damn stiff-collared Earp boys. Someday he'd blow that bragging Doc to the second Hell—the first wasn't far enough away for him. Then Brocius slammed his great hand at the saddlehorn. There would be no celebrating tonight in Rosa's cantina. He reached in the sagging pocket on his blue calico shirt and dug out a plug of Mule Ear Tobacco; then he cut off a chunk big enough to worm a full-size mule with the knife from his waistband. He applied the chew to his right jaw, and then chomped down on the hard twist to secure some of the juices to swallow. Narrow-eyed, he looked a last time to the north.

"Go get your horses. You can go back to the old man's ranch. I'm going back to Naco. You don't need to tell that old bastard a thing about this deal."

"Oh, *sí*, Señor Brocius," Obregon said, sounding relieved his life had been spared for another day.

Brocius reined his part-Percheron horse around and sent him off in a trot toward the south. The blazing sun danced on the mirages of lakes that flooded the San Bernadino. Weary of the trot, Brocius made the black horse lope. He needed lots of whiskey and his woman, so he could forget about this bad afternoon. Never again would he send for that haughty Stillwell or Reno. Piss on them. The next time he would get more of Old Man Clanton's regular cowboys to help him.

What next time? He had waited for three weeks to learn about the shipment of gold and silver bars that the stage contained. Some Mexican mining operation was sending it through Naco thinking that they could avoid the *banditos* that worked along the Santa Cruz River and the Camino Reale. His little whore Julia had learned about it from the mining company warehouse agent Phillipe, and then she had told Brocius all about it. Maybe that company would try it again. In an ordinary stage holdup in the valley, a robber would be lucky to take a brass watch and some coins from the passengers. The heavily guarded stages that traveled from Tombstone to Bisbee and on to Tucson left deep tracks from the silver bullion and the like that they carried out. By contrast, this twice-weekly line from the border to Fort Bowie, where it connected with the main line, barely made expenses, and certainly the front boot seldom held much of value.

Except for this day, and he had lost his chance through stupidity. With his large rowled spurs, he made the black run faster—hell with everyone, he was going to get mean drunk.

He gave the boy at the livery corral a dime to walk his lathered horse until he was cooled out, and then Brocius headed for Rosa's cantina. People saw the rage in his brown eyes and moved aside as he strode up the dusty street like a man on a mission. His shoulder parted the bat-wing doors, and he bellowed for Cortez to bring him a bottle. He spat his brown cud at a filthy spittoon, but it fell short and spotted the dirt floor in a trail, and even dripped off his matted black beard. Not bothering to wipe his tobacco-crusted lip, he beat on the first table with his ham of a fist.

"I want whiskey and by gawd I want it now!" he bellowed again.

"Coming, Señor Brocius," the small man said as he held the bottle high and came running from behind the bar with a glass in his other hand.

"Where is Julia?" Brocius asked, jerking the bottle from his grasp. Using his teeth, he extracted the cork and spat it at the man. Then he held the bottle raised in one hand and the glass in the other as he wondered about clapping his hands on both sides of the stupid Cortez's head. It might wake the stupid donkey.

"Asleep, I guess, señor."

"Go get her ass up. Tell her Brocius is back!"

"I will, señor!"

"Go do it now!" He sent the man reeling toward the curtained side doorway with a kick in the seat of his pants.

Cortez staggered a little from the blow, recovered, and then ran out of the barroom through the red curtains, and on down the inner hallway. Good enough for him. He would have her out there in a few minutes. Brocius was fed up with incompetent people—he raised the glass of brown liquor and silently toasted himself to better times. He would have them soon or he'd know the reason why. He itched to kill someone for causing this miserable day. Who should he kill? Maybe someone would come in the bar and insult him like that bucktoothed cowboy did in San Lucas, Texas. The punk kid had come in the Royal Palace Saloon, jerked some sweet girl off Brocius's lap, and said, "Come here, gal, to me. I've got a lot more to stick in you than that fat boy there has."

That beaver-faced kid found himself facing Brocius's pistol muzzle, and was soon stripping down to his pants and underwear. Then Brocius forced him to parade around stark naked at gunpoint to show his little shriveled-up root to everyone in the place.

Why, the puny thing wouldn't have filled a .44 gun barrel. Then Brocius kicked him out bare-ass into the street, and threw his clothes after him. In a short while, the kid came back all pumped up for a gunfight. Brocius rose up, shot him dead, and then had a swamper drag him out in the alley so his ugly face wouldn't disturb the barroom crowd. Even when he was dead, his front teeth stuck out like a rat's.

Brocius spent a week in jail and the jury came in hung. So that night he took his leave of the 'dobe jail, not waiting for a second chance to be tried, and rode over into New Mexico until things cooled down.

"Oh, Brocius." Julia swooned with her arms held out for him as she crossed the barroom in her low-cut silky dress to where he sat. Then she slipped into his lap and began to kiss him with her wet mouth.

His hand slid under her dress and ran up her silky legs. His heart quickened at the discovery she wore no underwear. She raised her butt on one side, then the other as she parted her legs and then winked at him.

"My, my, you are in big hurry, dear."

His thumb parted her wet gates and at his entry, she clutched his head with both of her small hands. A slow smile crossed his mouth as he sought her with his index finger. He would have her hotter than a ripe chili pepper when he took her back there to the crib. The stage robbery might have gone wrong, but this wouldn't. He reached behind her back with his other hand, lifted the glass, and tossed the liquor down. The fiery mescal cut a trail down his throat and warmed his ears.

"Ah, Brocius," she sighed, and looked dreamy-eyed at him as his pumping finger sought her deeper and she widened her legs for him. Her soft cooing of pleasure in his ear stirred him to work faster. Her small breasts rose and fell under the low-cut dress front. He needed to suck one.

"Stick one of them tits out for me," he said.

"Here?" she asked blinking in disbelief.

"Here," he insisted with a frown.

"This one?" she asked as she pushed down the material for him, but he had already lowered his mouth to the quarter-size nipple. His hungry quest of the small circle of flesh made her cry out.

3

"A *tigre*, señor?" Tomas asked as he ran his hand over the pelt that Slocum handed to him. His horse fidgeted under him, but he checked him, intrigued by the trophy. The man had brought Slocum's bay horse back when he came to check up on him.

"And I want to go back and get this buck's horn," Slocum said, handing the sheep carcass from behind his neck to Tomas. The man spread it over his lap. Then Slocum took the reins as the bay snorted through his nose at the smell of the jaguar's hide and the strong odor of the butchered ram.

"He sure don't like them tigers," Slocum said, setting the stirrup to mount. "But I never even suspected that there was one in a hundred miles. That tiger and I argued over the sheep a minute or two."

"All my life I have heard of the *tigre*, but this is the first one I ever see." Tomas shook his head in disbelief.

"They must be very rare this far north. They have lots of them down in the jungles," Slocum said stepping up. Once he was aboard, the bay tried to shy, but this time Slocum was ready and spurred the horse in place.

"You have been down there?" Tomas asked. "Where they live at?"

"Once."

"What was it like, señor?"

15

"Many trees, hot and humid, you sweat a lot. There are javelinas, monkeys, funny-colored parrots, and plenty of snakes to bite you. Leeches in the rivers to suck your blood."

"Oh." Tomas shook his head in distaste. "I will take the desert then."

"Me too." Slocum agreed, taking the skin back and fighting with his snorty horse as he did.

"Are you going after the horns?"

He reconsidered. "No, it's getting late. Besides, I don't have a place to keep them anyway."

"Vasquez will be proud of this sheep."

"He's always proud of meat to cook. Any trouble today?"

"No. We had to exchange an ox who got lame, but we still have three extras."

"No Indians?"

"I saw no sign."

"I hope we don't see any. Let's get back to camp." Slocum studied the sun's position in the west. Perhaps five o'clock or so. He must have carried the sheep carcass, his rifle, and the smelly hide for several miles before Tomas came with his horse. A good thing for him that the pony had run north instead of south and gone to the wagons. Otherwise he'd still be afoot.

An hour later when they rode up to camp, he could see the oxen spread out grazing the wiry dried grass. The wagons were in a circle and the men were smoking pipes or corn shucks.

"Look, the *patron* has killed a *tigre*!" Tomas shouted to the others as he delivered the ram to the cook.

The men rushed over to stare at the smelly pelt Slocum tossed to them. They backed up and let it fall on the ground as if fearful it might harm them. Awed, they circled it, all afraid to touch it. Finally, one of the men picked it up and stroked it.

"It is very smooth," he told the others.

"Did it attack you, *patron*?"

"No, but we argued over that sheep I shot."

"There is an omen about one who kills the cat," the

one-eyed Huerro said. Despite his dead eyeball, shriveled and cast, he looked up at Slocum as if both his pupils had vision. "Do you know it?"

"What is that?"

"The slayer of the *tigre* will become a god of the thunderstorms." Everyone laughed at his words; more of the men were gaining their nerve and wished to handle the skin. They stepped in to pet it.

"Good, I will give you much rain in Sonora when I am in charge."

His words drew their laughter, an edgy worried-sounding chortle. He knew these people were suspicious and they had never seen a real *tigre* skin this fresh. They wondered if the consequences of such a kill would be good or bad. But he knew a man in Tucson who would treasure the skin for his restaurant wall, and Slocum would give it to him.

Tomas posted armed guards and issued each man a loaded Spencer or revolver. Many of the drivers carried their own cap-and-ball pistols of skeptical condition in holsters on their hips, but the new rifles had better range and were more reliable. Though the rim-fired cartridges were weak compared to a .50-caliber Hawkins muzzle-loader, the Spencer repeater carried a wallop. There was something about a new well-oiled rifle, Slocum mused over his steaming coffee as the long twilight settled on the camp. Such a weapon gave the holder confidence.

A coyote began to yip as he walked to the edge of the circle and considered the next two days until they reached Cienga. There would be little forage for the oxen in the region, and no water except that in their kegs, until they reached the tules and wetlands. Another desert dog joined the chorus, and their throaty wailing grew louder as the first stars flecked the sky. The day's heat would soon subside. The temperature must have been close to a hundred, not excessive for this land, which could roast a man's brain.

"No sign of those Indians?" Tomas asked.

"No sign. But they don't leave much either. They aren't liable to attack such a force as ours. They like smaller numbers and less suspicious travelers."

"I understand that we must be ready."

"No sign of the errant driver?"

"No, and no one knows where he was at."

"Someone knows." Slocum glanced back to the blazing fire and the men seated around it. Satisfied that they could not hear his words, he continued. "If he is alive, then he wanted his business kept a secret. Otherwise someone killed him for his money and big gold watch."

Tomas frowned in the light from the fire. "How much money could he have?"

"Enough to buy a bottle or a *puta*—who cares. In this land, life is cheap. You can hire a man to kill his own mother for ten centavos." Slocum drew a small cigar from his vest and then struck a match on the side of the wagon box. The cigar came to life, the tip glowing red, and he tasted the sweet smoke in his mouth. He blew the smoke out in a small stream. Not bad.

"I know what you mean, señor. Sometimes I wish I was at home at Hermosia."

"Why are you here then?"

"My father's hacienda is not that big and my older brother—"

"You don't have to say any more."

"Did you have one? An older brother?"

"No, I *was* one."

"Then why are you here?" Tomas frowned at him.

"War. It changed everything." Slocum half-closed his eyes. The last peach rouge of twilight settled on the Gulf of California. He could hear the cannons roar and the shouts of men, crazed men anxious to kill the enemy, anxious to die. But no Yankee lead had found him. It had found his best friends. He drew in the smoke and inhaled it deep inside his lungs. A bullet had found Jack Campbell—at Gettysburg on a hot day in June. They had been able to smell Washington, D.C., from there. He heard once again the drum of a thousand horses, artillery exploding all around, and the screams of men both dying and living.

The copper smell of blood and the sulphurous puke of a gun barrel were branded in his nostrils. Life had been cheap that day and many days after. The coyotes broke his thoughts as they yipped closer.

"Get some men with rifles—that ain't coyotes," he said to Tomas, and drew his Colt from his holster. "We've got company and it might get hair-raising."

"*Sí,*" and the man was gone. Slocum slipped from his position and dropped to a crouch behind the greasewood, trying to see an outline or silhouette in the night. His ears listened for the faint sound of leather soles on grit. Then someone ran to his left in the brush and he opened fire with the Colt while sprawling belly-down. His shots were placed, but anything could deflect them.

He drew a scream of pain that made him smile, and then, from his own men, more gunfire cut the night. He could see the red-orange streaks of the muzzle blasts as he fought the smaller .31 from his boot top and rolled aside so the raiders could only guess his position.

"Are you all right, señor?" Tomas asked from the wagons.

"Yes. I think they are going to their horses." He tried to hear the fleeting sounds in the distance. It sounded like one of the raiders fell into a dry wash and the others slid down after him. Then there were the sounds of fleeing horses in the distance.

"Those bloodthirsty dogs!" someone shouted. Cheers came from the camp, along with stinging insults about the raiders' ancestry and their sexual habits. Most certainly the men felt more confident having turned back the attack regardless of the number or the condition of the enemy.

"How did you know it wasn't coyotes?" Tomas asked, joining him.

"I think an angel told me or I had a hunch." Slocum squinted against the darkness, seeing only the outline of the towering saguaros and the mountains before them. His strong intuition had saved him before, and once again it had stepped in like a guardian angel and spared him and his men from a serious fate. How far had the Indians gone? Would they be back? There were lots of things he wanted an answer for as a real coyote yelped at the small moon rising over the crest above them.

A jaguar and an Indian attack all in one day. *Don Alvares, I'm coming, but it sure has started out tough.*

4

"What do you mean, he already knows of another gold shipment?" Brocius asked, lying on his back in her bed with his hands cupped under his head. A small sliver of reflected light shone in on the mud-waddle ceiling overhead as he studied it and waited for her return to the bed.

She came back, climbed onto the mattress beside him, and pressed her small naked body to his. She threw her small arm on top of his great chest and with her fingertips, twisted the thick forest of black hair on his chest into curls.

"You saying that asshole knows about another shipment?" he asked.

"Hush, someone will hear us," she scolded.

"How do you know that he knows?" he hissed.

"They have changed the law. Soon they can bring in gold and silver ore and not pay any money to the commissioner. What you call that, tariff?"

"Yeah, tariff. What does that have to do with him and a gold shipment?" The bed protested loudly as he rolled over on his side, almost crowding her out. Settled, he stared at her small form beside him in the semi-darkness, and then shoved her hand down to his root. She began to squeeze it and he smiled.

"Good girl. Now tell me about this gold business."

"He don't know what day yet, but in a month or so there

20

will be this new law and they will bring ore up here by the pack train.''

"Is it rich ore? I have no smelter.'' He pushed his hips toward her as her actions began to make his rod stiffen.

"At first it will be ore,'' she whispered. "Then, when the commissioner gets lax at searching their packs, they will ship their gold bars under the rocks.''

"How long will that be?'' he asked, still wondering when he could get a real shipment and not some damned old rocks.

"Not as long as you are,'' she said, holding his stiff rod up and then letting go. Like a flagpole it remained standing, and they both scrambled in the bed to get in position. The ropes protested and squeaked as he rose to his knees and she slipped underneath him.

Hardly thinking about her, he loomed over her as she spread her legs apart and he nosed his aching tool inside her gates. How did this dumb warehouse man Phillipe know so much? Brocius began to punch his way into her. A whole gold train—by gawd, he would never have to rustle any more Mexican cattle. Never have to live in such a squalid place like this jacale of hers. Why, for the rest of his life he could look up at those fancy tin-squared ceilings instead of mud and sticks.

She arched her back for more. He knew he was big this time, bigger than ever, and despite his last fluids being in her, he was giving her hell as he drove deeper and deeper and the resistance grew harder. His wrists ached supporting his great bulk over her small form as his butt pounded her.

Then she cried out in pleasure and began to rock under him. He couldn't afford to miss a big shipment of bullion. Her small fingers closed around his scrotum—damn, that felt good. Those Mexicans could never suspect he or any-one else knew a thing about their shipments, or they would be on their guard all the time. His heart was running a hundred miles an hour at the prospect of stacks of gold bars, and her contractions grew harder as he plunged deeper and deeper.

Who could he trust? No one. His breath raged in and out of his lungs. He would scout them by himself. Only at the very end would he enlist any help. What if others found out? He began to hunch faster. He would have to kill them. Maybe he should kill the freight agent so he could not talk to anyone else about the plan.

Julia was going to crush his balls in her fingers. Had she lost her mind? Gawdammit, he winced at the pain. She was hurting him.

"Don't!" he shouted, but then he knew her plan and his eruption came like fire. In a panic to catch the most of her, he drove himself to the bottom of her well before his fuse went off and he spent his seed out in a volcanic eruption that left him too weak to stay suspended above her.

My gawd, he would be rich, and it would not take long either. An entire gold train would be his for the taking. He would have plenty of time to decide where and when. This time it would not turn out like the fiasco of the stage robbery. She eased out from under him, and he collapsed with a squawk from the ropes under the thin mattress. Out of energy, too numb and drained to even think about his new plan, he pulled her to him and hugged her. His hand ran over her small butt and became familiar enough that she tried to scoot away from it.

He laughed at her as she looked indignantly at him for his action. Then she settled her head on his chest. He did not deserve a *puta* like Julia. His hand squeezed the left side of her small butt. Why, she understood him and liked him to do it to her. When he had money he lavished things on her, and when he was broke, she bought him whiskey and let him share her small casa and bed for free. Such a little one too, but she knew what to do. Damn, a whole gold train coming out of Mexico riding right into his arms.

In San Francisco, they said, they had whores that looked like queens. They probably cost fifty dollars a night. Shit, it was only damned old Mexican gold anyway. She finally crawled up and lay on top of his chest. Then, in submission, she spread her legs apart for his finger to probe inside her. Why, when he had all that gold, there was no telling what he might do.

5

The boy Miguel brought his saddled horse in the first light of dawn. There was no sign of the unseen Indians as the men yoked their animals, but Slocum felt anxious to check on any signs they'd left. He'd risen early that morning half-way expecting a dawn raid, but nothing had happened. That could mean no one was about, or that they had slipped in close under the cover of night to wait for enough light.

The Seris were not Apaches, who seldom struck at night for fear that if they were killed in the dark, their spirits would be doomed to walk the earth forever. Still, visibility was a good thing to have on your side when you charged a well-armed camp. When men first awoke was when they were the most vulnerable, and you could use the sun at your back to blind your enemy. Plains Indians used this technique well. Slocum listened as the desert birds began to tweet and whistle—another good sign. If the chaparral was full of raiders, they would be silent. Still, he wanted to ride out and make a wide circle to check for any signs.

He mounted the short bay horse smoothly. It was no doubt a mustang of the desert, but a tough wiry animal. Slocum would not have chosen it on first look, but he had learned the animal was tireless and nimble-footed, and he also knew that the little horse did not like *tigres*. He set the pony into a trot. With his hammer guard on his holster undone, he rose in the stirrups and entered the knee-high greasewood brush.

He found little sign, except for scuff marks in the bank where he'd thought they had escaped the night before. There were a few barefoot pony tracks in the dry wash sand, but they were soon lost. Maybe a half-dozen warriors. They were probably out on a raiding party and he had discouraged them. Good enough. He needed to get the train moving in the cool portion of the day so they could make it through the pass. He would have to scout that area too— it would be the best ambush site on their route.

"Anything?" Tomas asked, riding up on a sorrel pony to meet him.

"No, but we must scout the canyon ahead and be careful. I will be glad when we are on the other side." He looked around. The men seemed lethargic about getting ready. Would he never get use to their Latin ways?

"I will tell the men to hurry, señor," Tomas said, obviously reading the displeasure on his face.

"It might save their lives," he said. Then he rode to Vasquez's wagon and dismounted, and the snowy-bearded cook handed him a fresh cup of coffee.

"Well, were there a hundred or a few?" the man asked in Spanish.

"A few."

"That is why they did not return?"

"I think so. But I'll be glad when we're through the mountains."

"Maybe by mid-morning?" Vasquez asked.

"Yes. If we can get them to move." He gave a rueful look at the men about the camp. They were still taking their time about getting ready despite Tomas's shouting.

"Oh, Captain, we will be through the mountains by then. I will spread the word the Seris have gone back for more men."

"*Gracias, amigo,*" Slocum said with a grin, and toasted him with the steaming tin cup.

Vasquez's rumor spread like wildfire. By the time Slocum's coffee had cooled enough to only burn his tongue and not sear it, the camp was in an uproar. Finished, he handed the empty cup back with a grin and a soft thank-you to Vasquez. He remounted the bay and rode to the front.

"I will scout ahead. You be careful and keep your eyes open," he warned Tomas when he drew his horse up.

"Fine, I will watch. I don't know what came over the men, but they are sure getting ready," Tomas said.

"A good boss can do anything," he said to the younger man.

Tomas did not look as if he believed the words. Slocum took his leave and rode ahead into the canyon. For perhaps three miles the wagon road was chiseled out of the red rock as it wound up a deep canyon, over the grade, and then downhill to spill out in the desert. There was not much cover on the slopes, which meant that attackers would have to conceal themselves high above. But arrows fell, and they could make the train a pincushion in no time and then slip down to finish off the survivors.

An echo of the bay's iron shoes on the rocks reverberated from the steep walls that towered above him. Slocum searched the sun-clad slopes as he rode in the cool shadows. The trail twisted around a bend as his horse snorted softly in weariness. Slocum wondered if there was an armed savage waiting when he made the turn. But there was only more of the crude narrow road gaining height as it snaked upward to the pass.

He craned his neck to see where there might be a potential ambusher above him, and then he listened. An eagle or hawk screamed overhead. Slocum wet his lip. Then the shadow of the gliding bird of prey passed over him and he knew the call was a real one. His heart eased.

In the pass, he let the wind sweep his face and the huffing pony caught his breath. He could see the rest of the Terra Baldinas, a vast flat desert basin that swept to the east until haze obscured his view. It was an arid land which did not forgive men. Many bones were bleached in the dry washes.

A pair of buzzards circled far out. There was something dead, for they obviously were appraising an object worthy of eating. He looked over the barren red rock formations worn smooth by the winds of time. There was no sign that an Indian or even a lizard stirred. That suited him fine. Two days without water, and then they would be to Cienga. It was a perilous way to travel—any delay en route would tax man and beast—but this dim road was the shortest route from the sea to Tucson. It was not as bad as the longer route across from Yuma, and besides, the riverboats charged too much to bring the freight up the Colorado River from the Gulf.

He set the bay off the mountainside toward the desert below. His back muscles eased a little. What held the black carrion birds' interest? They must be having a feast on something. He trotted the bay. Anything dead was unusual enough to investigate.

He found a dead horse lying sprawled in the road. Feasting buzzards flapped their great wings and left their meal at his approach. The animal's hide had been peeled back in a crude fashion to cut out portions of meat from his leg. Slocum drew his Colt and looked about at the towering saguaros and the weeping paloverdes. The dead horse was still saddled and he could see where a bridle had been stripped. The salt marks of the headgear showed on the agonized-looking face of the dead animal. A buzzard had already plucked out its eyeball. No doubt the horse had died in pain.

Slocum dismounted and, gun in hand, searched about for the rider. Then the squawk of more buzzards arguing over something else sent him down the hillside. Through the brush, he spotted a snow-white body on the ground, and in his anger he fired at the black birds desecrating it. The screams of panic-stricken buzzards and the beating of their great wings filled the air as he rushed down the gravel slope on his boot heels.

Too late, of course. The naked body had been staked out on its back. A young man of thirty or so, or what remained of him after torture and mutilation. His mouth was wide open. He had no doubt died screaming. Slocum closed his eyes at sight of the dried bloody wound where his manhood should be. The Seris had done a thorough job on him. Burns showed on his body and face where they had branded him. What sort of person could get pleasure out of inflicting such pain? Slocum turned away. How could he cover him? They had taken every scrap of the poor devil's clothing, and by himself Slocum could hardly manage to move the horse's remains to get to the saddle blanket.

His bedroll tarp would have to be the man's shroud. He holstered his revolver after spinning the cylinder back in place so the hammer rested on an empty chamber. He had three shots left. En route to the horse, he cursed the persistent buzzards. They had to survive too, he decided, reaching the bay, but he still hated their desecration of the man. Soon he would have him wrapped up, and a detail from the wagon train could bury him.

Who was he? An American, no doubt. The man had short sandy hair. Perhaps Slocum would never know. He undid the lacing, careful to listen—the damn savages might come back. One dead gringo, no identification, nothing. He was surprised that they had left his saddle, but the weight of the horse upon it might have surpassed their strength to uncover it. They'd taken meat from it to cook, no doubt, and for another meal on the trail.

Men had done the butchering. Any Indian woman would have been neater; even in haste, she would not have managed such a crude job. Young boys probably, out testing their manhood—the worst kind for the unfortunate victim to meet up with. Slocum hurried back with the canvas wrap—a grisly job, but someone had to do it.

"The men will bury him," Tomas said later after Slocum had explained his gruesome find to the man. He had ridden back to be certain that the train came through the pass safely. There was no sign of the Seris, and while the skin on the back of his neck crawled, Slocum felt the young bucks had not wanted to take on so many armed men. As the lead wagon rolled through the pass, he felt more comfortable.

He turned the bay horse as the first wagon finally spilled out on desert floor to follow the dim tracks that led northeastward. In a long trot, he set out to check on Cienga— or the Tules, as some called the place. He passed the nameless man's dead horse and scattered the great birds. A shame there was no next of kin to notify. They would have to wonder forever what had happened to him. Slocum rode on.

In mid-afternoon, he halted the winded pony and let him breathe. In the distance, a few gnarled cottonwoods held up their yellow leaves, the only splash of color in the drab brown desert scene. They marked the site of the water hole. Places like this attracted the good and the bad. It was the only source of the precious liquid for fifty miles. He stood in the stirrups and observed with caution the thin smoke.

Someone was camped there. He undid the thong on his six-gun, drew it, and checked the loads. Since firing at the buzzards earlier, he had reloaded it, but it paid to be certain when one might be dealing with Indians or outlaws. To live in this thorny land you had to be the last one standing. He intended to continue his life.

There were four men around the fire, and a Mexican woman in a *reboza* squatted down stirring the fire and cooking something. From under their wide sombreros, he saw their hard eyes and contemptuous looks. One man rose. He wore a bandolier, the loops half filled with mixed ammunition.

"Ah, señor," the man said, pushing his hat back and eyeing Slocum's horse and equipment as if he intended to be the new owner.

"Good afternoon," Slocum said, watching the other three fish-eyed *vaqueros*.

"Come join us, we were just having some tea," the man offered.

"I might do that," Slocum said, trying to make sure that there wasn't another slipping around behind him.

"Something is wrong, señor?" the leader asked, smoothing his thick mustache with the top of his hand.

"I don't reckon." Slocum dropped from the saddle, adjusted the Colt out of habit, and then led the pony over.

"You must ride from Libertad."

"I've been there. You know of any gringo that rode through here, say, a day ago?"

"No. Why?"

"The Seris killed a man about fifteen miles west of here on the road."

"We saw no one. How did you manage to live if they killed him?" The man frowned, and the others listened closely for any information on the feared Indians.

"They were gone when I rode through," Slocum said after thanking the hard-looking woman for the pottery cup of hot tea. "I found him staked out."

He cupped the warm vessel in his hand. The men acted in no hurry to jump him, though he distrusted the four of them. Gut feelings meant a lot, and no one knew that better than Slocum. He didn't wonder if they would try to rob him. The only question was when. These were desperate men in an equally hostile land.

"Did you see these Seris?" the older man with the knife scar on his cheek asked.

"I saw their butchery."

"They tortured him, huh?" the leader asked as they stood about drinking the sharp tea.

"He died in pain, let's say that."

"What is your business in this land, gringo?" the leader asked.

"I have many businesses," Slocum said.

"Ah, a rich man. My name is Cruz. You ever heard of me?"

"Never had the privilege before. My name is Slocum."

"Oh, Señor Slocum. What does such a rich Americano do in these desolate lands?"

"Mind my own business."

"Did you pass a wagon train coming through the mountains?"

"No," Slocum lied.

"*Mierda*! It is suppose to come soon." The leader shook his head in grim disapproval.

"You have business with them?" Slocum asked.

"Were they still at Libertad waiting for a ship?"

"A bunch of wagons and carts?"

"Oh, *sí*. They are still there?" Cruz's thick eyebrows formed a hood over his inquiring dark eyes.

"When I left the drivers were all raising hell in the whorehouses and cantinas," Slocum said to test their intentions, though he felt sure larceny lurked in their minds.

"Such a miserable place," Cruz said in disgust. "I wonder where the ship is."

"Who knows about ships? Maybe they wrecked coming around the Horn." Slocum handed the empty cup back to the woman and dismissed her offer to refill it. They obviously waited there to rob his wagon train; they sure weren't there to hand out bibles.

"You are right. What do caballeros know of such things?" The man laughed aloud.

"I plan to water my horse," Slocum said, feeling the others were only waiting for a word from Cruz to pounce on him.

"Water your fine steed," Cruz said as if he owned the watering hole. "Then come back and we will talk more. I have a proposition for you."

"Oh?" Slocum asked, and stopped to turn back and look at the man.

"It can wait," Cruz said, waving him on.

The others looked away when he checked them. Satisfied the moment had passed, he set out in the loose sand for the tank. Obviously the woman or someone had drawn enough water from the hand-dug well, for the rock and mortar trough was half full. Slocum filled his canteen as the bay drank deep, the slugs of water rippling down his throat. At last Slocum felt satisfied the men weren't sneaking up on him, and he bent over and drank his fill of the warm water.

Wiping his mouth with his kerchief, he wondered how Cruz planned to take the wagon train. He loosened the cinch as he tried to picture the layout of the land. He needed to know more about the four men too. The acrid whiff of the campfire carried on the hot wind as he led the bay back up the sandy draw.

"How much money you got, Slocum?" Cruz asked as he shoved a white woman toward him. "I want to sell her."

She was in her twenties, thin, her dark brown hair in a bun and very disheveled. Obviously she had been crying, for her downcast eyes were red. Dirty streaks marked her tear-stained face. The blue dress was filthy and several of the top buttons were gone, allowing the white skin that separated her small breasts to show.

"Who is she?" Slocum asked as the woman, standing ten feet from him, looked away.

"Señora McCoy is her name."

"How did you get her?" Slocum asked.

"We found her," Cruz said, and the others laughed aloud. They shared some private joke about her, nodding their heads. At this point, Slocum needed little imagination to realize what they had done to her.

"This man is a—an animal," she said in English, and raised her chin.

"He is also very dangerous," Slocum said through his teeth. "I am not certain what I can do. But I will try not to let them hurt you anymore."

She nodded to indicate that she had heard him.

"What did she say in English, Slocum?" Cruz asked, swaggering past her.

"She said you were a *mucho hombre*. A real stallion—" Slocum's left hand shot out to grasp the grinning outlaw as his right hand drew his Colt and he rammed the muzzle into the man's gut. His fist wrapped around a bandolier, he dragged Cruz in close to his face. "Tell them to throw down their pistols or I'm making a new window in your stomach."

6

Billy Dale Spears came looking for Brocius on Friday. The Texas cowboy rode up and dropped off his horse in front of Rosa's cantina. He undid his cinch, hitched his reins, then looked around at the half-dozen goats being driven through the dusty street by some boys. Then the bandy-legged Texan ducked around the hitch rail and came up on the shaded porch.

"What the hell are you drinking, Brocius?" Spears asked.

"Cactus piss. Have a damn seat. What brings you to this shit pot on the border?" Brocius reached over and poured some mescal in the spare glass.

"The old man sent me. We need you to help us."

"What are you doing?"

"Hell, the old man's got beef contracts to fill."

"Rustling again, huh?" Brocius settled back in the wicker chair. The porch was shaded by the palm fronds piled on top, and offered a cool spot for him to drink and observe anything that happened in the dried-up little border village.

He was glad to see a friend who talked English. To have someone besides the damn braying donkeys and bleating goats to listen to. He sat back to listen. So Old Man Clanton needed him. Good, that meant money and he always needed money, especially since the stage robbery attempt had failed so miserably.

"You didn't think the old man was going to buy beef, did you?"

"Hell, no, not when he could steal them for a lot less." Brocius laughed aloud.

"He wants us ready to ride in the morning."

Brocius studied the pottery cup in his hand. That meant he'd have to start out soon to be ready in the morning. Damn, he hated to leave his little darling Julia. But there was nothing he could do but ride out there and stay at the old man's all night. Having some cash was better than being broke and mooching off his *puta*.

"Here." He poured more liquor in the cowboy's cup.

"This stuff will bite you," Spears said with a shake of his head.

"Hell, it's real mild. They make some of this mescal out of hot peppers that will build a real fire in you."

"They got food in there?" Billy asked with a head toss.

"Sure," Brocius said. "Hey, Peppe!"

A young man in a white apron appeared, wiping his hands on the cloth. *"Sí, señor."*

"Bring us some food."

"Good, 'cause I need to eat something," Billy said. "This damn mescal's making me light-headed already."

Peppe returned with two bowls of rice and beans. Chunks of meat and tomatoes swam in the mixture. He left them a stack of corn tortillas, and Brocius nodded in approval.

Billy dipped out a tortilla full of the mixture, and with a smear of red over his mouth nodded in approval. "Good."

Few words were shared as the pair devoured the mixture and the stack of tortillas. Brocius wondered where the old man intended to rustle the herd from this time, but there were plenty of vulnerable ranches south of there. Old Man Clanton knew all of them. Why, he'd even moved down to Sonora from Arizona to set himself up better and not have so far to ride when he went out to steal.

They finished off another bottle of mescal in the shade of the porch while observing the town's women passing by, with a private word or wink shared between them on the

beauty or ugliness of each one. Finally Brocius drew himself up, went inside, and found Julia. He told her of their
plans, kissed her good-bye and then got his big horse from
the corrals. Then he and Spears rode out to Clanton's headquarters.

Near dark, they dismounted at the pens. A Mexican boy
took their mounts and they headed for the long rambling
ranch house. Brocius took off his hat and wiped his forehead on his sleeve. He studied the crimson glow in the
west. His belly growled and he wondered if there was any
food left. He slapped on his big hat and followed Spears
to the washing facilities set out on the table under the long
porch.

They washed up and then dried their hands and faces on
the coarse towels, returning them to the rack. Their spurs
jangling, they went down the dirt porch and inside the
lighted doorway.

"About time you two got here," Old Man Clanton said
from behind a spoon held close to his shaggy gray beard.
His bald head shone under the lighted lamp hung above the
great table. Then, as if satisfied with his comments, he
dropped his gaze to the soup in the spoon and slurped it
up.

"Good see you," Brocius said to the old man, and then
moved to the empty chairs on the end. He received grunts
and greetings from the other cowboys as he seated himself.

"What took you so gawdamn long to get here?" the old
man demanded. His words silenced the talking around the
table.

Brocius shrugged. "Had to ride out here."

"I was going to get me someone else."

'Sorry about that, sir. I was coming as soon as Billy Dale
here found me."

"They say you got some hot pussy in Naco." Clanton's
words drew a titter of laughter from the men up and down
the long table. Looks were shot at Brocius as they waited
for his reply.

"Aw, Clanton, you know how those rumors get started,"
Brocius said, and shook his head to dismiss any concern.

"They tell me, Bill, that you are robbing stages these

days.'' The old man picked around in his soup with the spoon. His teeth were too broken and rotten to chew solid food, so he always ate liquid meals.

"Whenever I can stop one."

"We heard about that. How much money was on that stage?" The old man leaned forward to hear his words.

"Maybe a couple of hundred," Brocius lied with a shrug, and began to fill his plate. It was none of the old man's damn business how much money he'd missed. It was well known, he felt certain, that the box held over a thousand. He wouldn't be so willingly doing the old man's bidding if he'd gotten the money.

"You'll make more than that working for me. Why were you risking getting your dumb ass blowed off by some stagecoach guard?"

"I guess I was restless." Brocius filled his plate with slabs of fried steaks from the platter handed him by some of the others, and dipped out fluffy white rice from a large pan passed to him. Then the pigtailed Chinese cook handed him a hot bowl of fresh gravy. Waiting for more questions from Clanton, he busied himself buttering some fried bread. The old man wanted American food, so there was little of the Mexican cuisine that the cook specialized in.

"Restless, huh, boys? Curly Bill's restless." Clanton dropped his head in disapproval and spooned in some more of his soup with a loud slurp. Then, with his mouth full, he waved the spoon. "Tomorrow I'll take that all out of him."

The others laughed up and down the table. Even one-eyed Perkins laughed, and Brocius felt embarrassed being chided like that by the old man. If anyone else had done that, he'd have shot them on the spot. But Old Man Clanton was the reason he was in Arizona. He'd been pretty reckless growing up in Texas, and was sitting in a jailhouse awaiting trial when he first saw the bearded patriarch of the Clanton clan. Clanton walked up and hung on the bars of his cell, dressed in a threadbare old suit with his gray beard like a bib. He asked Brocius his name.

"They call me Curly Bill Brocius," he answered, wondering if the old man was a preacher there to pray for his soul. All he needed was some damnation preacher saving his soul before they hung him.

"Then get off you ass, Brocius." With that said, the old man unlocked the cell and motioned impatiently for him to hurry. Brocius almost forgot his hat.

"Where's Rufus?" he asked, hurrying after Clanton. There was no sign of the deputy in the outer office as they hurried outside into the bright sunshine.

"He's locked up in the crapper," Clanton said as he nodded for Brocius to take the bay horse at the hitch rack.

Brocius looked all around as he swung in the saddle. The street was deserted. From out in back of the adobe jailhouse, he could hear Rufus Manning swearing and kicking at the outhouse's wooden walls. Why, he'd know that loud voice anywhere. How had they trapped the lawman in the outhouse? Then Ike Clanton, the old man's boy, came around the corner on a big chestnut and the three of them left Morgansville at a high lope.

So he owed the old man. Chances were that the jury they were calling in for his trial would have hung him or sent him to Huntsville for twenty years. The trouble had started when he'd shot three Mexicans over a mule they'd stolen from him. But the Texas law wasn't holding him for killing the three Mexicans. He was in jail for stealing the mule from a white man to start with.

He had ridden with the old man ever since. Clanton paid him well—the old man always paid him well. The only problem was, there wasn't enough work to support his habits like drinking and screwing whores all the time. So he often got restless.

Some of the others excused themselves from the supper table and tromped out of the room, until only Billy Dale, the old man, and Brocius were left. The old man was drinking good whiskey by then, and he never offered any to the others.

"We need about five hundred head of grown stock, fat enough to butcher," Clanton said aloud.

"That's a big number to simply rustle up," Brocius said, refilling his plate for the third time. He had lots of eating to do. The next week they'd probably eat jerky, crackers, and cheese and drink alkali water.

"I figure we make a sweep south down the Baranacas. There are enough small ranchers in that country, we can find all the cattle we need in a week."

"We ride south then and start back?" Brocius asked.

"Maybe split up. You and some of the boys go up the east fork. Me and the other half of the hands go up the main river."

"What if we get too many head?"

"We'll cull them."

"Who you giving me?" Brocius asked while wolfing down more gravy, steaks, and rice.

"Billy Dale?"

"Fine," he said between bites.

"Perkins, Rowdy, Vaught, McKelvey, and Raul. That good enough?"

Brocius stopped and considered the list. He knew Billy Dale was a good enough hand. Rowdy was a wet kid, Vaught a tough from Texas, and Raul knew the country. But he hated Perkins.

"You take that one-eyed bastard Perkins with *you*." He waved his fork at the old man between bites.

Clanton shook his head. "He goes with you."

"I don't like him."

"Too bad. He does his share." The words were final, and Brocius knew he would never change the old man's mind. He was stuck with the little bastard. Gawdamn, he hated that.

7

"Cruz, you move one damn inch, you're dead!" Slocum ordered as he used the man for a shield against the others with the muzzle of his Colt stuck hard in the outlaw's stomach. His left hand grasped the bandolier and kept Cruz close enough that he could smell the liquor on his breath. "Tell them to throw down their irons or I'm making daylight in your gut."

"Do as he says!" Cruz shouted.

"Don't hesitate!" Slocum warned them.

"Do it now!" Cruz seethed. "Who are you, hombre?"

"The man in charge of that wagon train that you were waiting to rob." He watched the others moving to obey him. The white woman staggered aside as if she were in a dream, and blinked in disbelief at the situation.

"You will never reach Nogales alive," Cruz snarled.

"My friend, you may have seen it for the last time." Slocum watched the others drop their weapons on the ground and then raise their hands. He doubted they were completely disarmed by any means—he felt certain they had hidden weapons—but they'd put down all the armaments that he could see.

"Take the gringo woman and ride. I can pay you much in gold," Cruz said.

"Looks to me like I have her and your gold." He jerked

the pistol from Cruz's holster with his left hand, tossed it aside, then shoved the man backward.

"I have many friends that will—"

"Shut up," Slocum said, wondering how he would hold them until his men arrived. "All of you sit down. Try something and you're dead.

"Get me some rope," he said to the stunned woman.

She blinked her violet eyes at him. Either she had not heard him, or else she was in a state of shock from their mistreatment of her, for she stood unmoving. There was no way that she could ever hold a gun on them. He had a mess on his hands.

"Ma'am," he said loudly. "Go get me a rope so I can tie them up!"

"Tie them up," she mumbled through her thin lips.

"Yes, I need a rope." He stopped and listened—someone was riding off on a horse. The other female, the Mexican woman who'd given him tea earlier, was streaking out of there on horseback. Damn, why hadn't he thought of her? Who could she bring down on them? Probably more riffraff like Cruz. The border swarmed with such two-bit bandits.

"Ha. Maria rides for my *compadres*. Your days are numbered now," Cruz said with such confidence that he sent cold chills up Slocum's spine. There was no way that she could ever reach anyone before his own men arrived. But he gave another shudder despite the heat, and then straightened his shoulders.

"I need a rope from one of their horses," he repeated to the thin woman.

She looked at him blankly and then nodded that she understood. Relieved, he watched her hurry in a pigeon-toed gait toward the animals. He focused his attention back to the seated outlaws. His heartbeat raged in his chest as he considered how to handle them. This had been too close for comfort. Riding in so openly could have led to his own demise. Who was the woman and what had they done to her?

She returned with two reatas—braided rawhide lariats that the *vaqueros* used. He forced the youngest one to lie facedown on the ground, and then laid the pistol on the ground beside his knee in case they tried anything as he tied the youth's hands tight behind his back. Forced to cut the tail of the raeta off to have enough for the others, he used his jackknife to slice through the tough leather. Then, rope and gun in hand, he jerked the next outlaw aside.

Cruz acted for a moment as if he might challenge him. For a long twenty seconds the outlaw looked ready to charge him. Slocum picked up his Colt and cocked the hammer. He waited for Cruz to try something. It would damn sure be his last try.

"You want to die on the sand between us?" Slocum finally asked the man.

"You will die soon enough," Cruz said, and settled on his butt.

At last, when all of them were belly-down in the dirt, their hands and feet bound, he stood up and holstered his pistol.

"What is your name?" Slocum asked the dazed woman.

"Audrey McCoy," she finally replied. There was something about the blank look in her eyes. He wondered what sort of hell she'd seen at the outlaws' hands.

"My husband Roger has gone for help," she managed, and then tears forced her to turn away.

"Did he ride southwest?"

"Yes," she sobbed.

He rubbed his stubbled mouth with the side of his index finger and wondered how to tell her. The only gringo he'd seen in three weeks besides the captain was a dead man. A man who had been tortured and killed by savages and who his men had planted in a shallow grave earlier that day.

"Mrs. McCoy?"

"Yes?"

"I fear that I have some bad news for you."

"What?" She batted her wet lashes at him.

"I fear that Indians killed your husband."

"Killed Roger! Oh, no!" Then her face drained of color. Slocum rushed in and caught her as she fainted. Her slender form limp in his arms, he looked around for a place to lay her down. He carried her to where several blanket rolls lay beyond the fire, and kicked one open. As gently as he could, he placed her on the blanket.

"No more," she mumbled with a pained look on her face as she turned from him. "Please don't rape me again."

"No one is going to touch you," he said, looking hard at his trussed-up outlaws on their bellies beyond the fire. What had they done to her?

"Please don't!" She held her hands up to protect her face and continued to look away. Her thin shoulders shook as she choked on her emotions.

"They won't touch you again, ma'am. You rest there." He rose, not knowing another thing he could do for the distraught woman. She'd been raped, by God only knows how many of these outlaws, and now she'd learned that her husband was dead. She would have to cry her way out of it. Obviously she didn't want to be held by a stranger.

Slocum had a large knot in his throat. He fought an impulse to go kick the blazes out of the outlaws. Anyone who abused a defenseless woman like her ought to be hung by the balls or have cactus spines stuck in his manhood. He left her and searched among their things for anything he could learn about the outlaws, not expecting to find much.

When his temper was under control, he went to the youngest one and jerked him up by his hair so his chest was off the sand. Slocum's words were in Spanish.

"Who raped her?" he shouted close to the youth's ear.

"Not me!"

"Who raped her?"

"Cruz and the others. You're hurting me." The boy's eyes were open wide, and he looked about ready to cry as Slocum held him by a fistful of his hair.

"What did you do, hold her down?"

"*Sí.* What will you do with us?"

"Castrate all of you." Slocum slammed his face down in the sand. He rose up to his feet and looked to the south. The rising dust of the wagon train hung in the south sky. They were coming. They'd arrive there in a few hours.

He crossed the camp to where she lay drawn up in a ball. Lowering himself down, he sat beside her. Maybe there was some comfort he could give her.

"In a short while, my wagon train will be here," he said softly. "Why don't you wash your face and comb your hair."

She blinked up at him and then raised up on her elbows. "I'm sorry, sir. I can't tell who is a friend or an enemy."

"The enemy is tied up." He tossed his head in the outlaws' direction. "I'll take them to the authorities in Nogales. Where do you need to go from here?"

"Nowhere. My life is over." She dropped her head and shook it as if lost.

"Mrs. McCoy, you're a young woman. You will have to pick up the pieces. Life has dealt you a stiff hand, but you have to go on living. Do you have family?"

"Kansas, I guess."

"Good, we'll get you to Tucson. From there you can take the stage to El Paso, and from there the train to Fort Worth and then go home."

She shook her head, not looking up. "I can't go home, Mr. Slocum."

"Slocum's fine. Why not?"

"I eloped with Roger and my father never approved of him or me doing such a thing."

"Sounds strange, but you don't know how good kinfolks, even unforgiven kinfolks, look coming back home."

"No." She sank down and buried her face in her sleeve. "I can't ever go home."

"Then in Tucson we will find you a job teaching school."

"Teaching school?" She sat up and looked at him perplexed.

"It's honest work. You sure don't want to go to work in some house of ill repute."

She looked away, and the red of embarrassment flushed her face. "I probably belong there."

"No one belongs there, unless they choose it."

"Who are you, Slocum?" she asked, peering at him.

"A man that your mamma warned you about to be sure and avoid."

"You have saved me from these, ah, outlaws, and now you intend to run my life?"

"No, ma'am, I won't do that," he said, feeling uncomfortable at her accusations, and started to rise. All he wanted to do was get her to survive.

Her hand shot out and stopped him. "Hold me. I think I may explode if you don't."

"Sure, gal. We have plenty of time to settle your new place in life." He reached out and pulled her on his lap.

She inhaled deeply, closed her wet eyelashes, and then nestled her face into his shirt. She was so thin and narrow, why, his arms almost circled her twice. He looked down at the dust that streaked down her chest where her dress fell open. He'd held lots of women in pleasure and to comfort them, but she was not receptive to his arms despite her asking to be held. She was indifferent to his embrace, he could feel, despite his attempt to console her. She had been through too much, the rape and her husband's demise. What would he do with her?

The loud squeak of the wooden carts was the first sound he heard, then bullwhips cracking and the cursing of men. She had taken his advice and washed in the tank before they arrived. With her hair back in a small bun and wearing a clean brown dress with a high collar, she had a fresh look that made him nod in approval when she came from behind the head-high cluster of organ-pipe cactus.

"Señor?" Tomas asked, frowning at the bound outlaws when he rode in camp. "Who are these hombres?"

"Robbers waiting for the train."

"You captured all of them by yourself?"

Slocum nodded as others rushed over and stared at the outlaws belly-down on the ground.

"That one is Cruz!" one of the men said, pointing at the leader. "He kidnapped my sister once." Only Tomas's quick action, catching the driver's arm, saved Cruz from receiving the man's wrath. The drivers and workers swept off their sombreros at the sight of the woman as they lined up and studied the bandits, talking softly.

"You will never reach Nogales unless you release me!" Cruz shouted.

His words drew nervous laughter from the crew. Then

they nudged each other with elbows and grinned as if satisfied that they knew what would really happen.

"What a rooster," someone shouted. "He is tied up for the picking and he still thinks he is cock of the yard."

"Señor?" Vasquez asked with his arms folded on his chest. "What will we do with such trash? These men are known killers and have raped the sisters of many of the men here."

"In Nogales—" Slocum began, but he stopped when he saw the men shake their heads grimly.

"Jails don't hold men like Cruz," Vasquez said.

Tomas agreed. "Why, he would buy his way out of jail in a second."

"Is the verdict in?" Slocum asked, looking the men over. From left to right, each one gave an affirmative nod. He realized their intentions and glanced over at the woman. She did not need to see this hand played out. "Let me take Señora McCoy away then."

They all agreed.

"Where are we going?" she asked. Obviously she had not understood the words in Spanish he had spoken with his men. He escorted her from the camp. Cruz began to scream in protest as they dragged him to his feet. He would be the first.

"You can't do this to me!" the outlaw screamed. "All of you will die for this!"

"The law of the road has spoken," Slocum said softly. He herded her past the water tank so she would not have to watch the executions. "They wish to hang them for their past outlaw ways."

"Is that legal?" she asked with a frown, trying to look back.

"Things are very harsh in this land. Those men did rape you." He turned her to the north and made her walk on.

"Yes, but the law . . ." She dropped her head.

"There is no law here. If they are guilty, then I have no right to stop this. Those men will get what they deserve. You were not their first victim either. Some of my men knew of them and what they did to their sisters and women."

"Should I be happy then?"

"No, it isn't enough for what they did to you just to give up their worthless lives," he said, and hugged her to his chest.

"No, it isn't." Her tears soaked his shirt as he stood in the bright sun holding her and listened to the slap on a horse butt and the sharp whang of a stretched reata thrown over a stiff cottonwood limb. There was no more vocal protesting from the leader. *Don Alvares, the train is coming. Damn, it's not an easy road back.*

8

Brocius rushed around the corner of the adobe and captured the screaming woman by her bare arms. One look down at her low-cut blouse and firm breasts and he knew what he would do with her. He'd sent Vaught to check on the out-building for any sign of resistance. The rest of the men were gathering cattle; he had enough time to mess with her.

"The rest of them are either dead or gone," Vaught said as he came around the adobe structure on horseback. Then he saw the woman that Brocius held by the arm, and a wide grin formed on his thin lips. "Say, she ain't half bad-looking."

"Not bad," Brocius agreed. "Hitch my horse around there. I'll be catching up with you and the boys in a little while."

"Sure thing, Boss." Vaught looked hard at the wide-eyed woman, no doubt wanting some of her flesh too. Too bad. Brocius watched him ride off. Then he shoved her inside the open doorway. Her upper arm held tight in his fist, he looked around for the nearest bed. In the corner he spied a large four-poster bed piled high with blankets.

"Don't hurt me," she said under her breath as he propelled her across the room.

"Hell, I ain't going to hurt you." He laughed aloud, and had to control himself when he shoved her up against the bed so she couldn't flee. "I'm going to make love to you. Get them clothes off."

She hesitated, and he snatched her up toward his face. "Get undressed!"

"*Sí,*" Her hands shook as she stripped off her blouse, and he admired her full breasts. Then, with a worried glance at him and after a moment's hesitation, she hurriedly pushed down her cotton skirt.

"You ain't half bad-looking," he said, hanging his holster on the chair back. Then he admired her fleshy legs and slightly bulging belly as he undid his fly. His mind awhirl with his plans for her, he shoved down his pants.

Her gaze dropped to the sight of his erect manhood, and her face paled at the sight.

"You are a *mucho* stallion," she gasped.

"Aw, honey, he ain't half hard yet. Get up on that bed." Like a crayfish on her butt, she moved quickly to obey him, the fear-filled stare directed at his stiffening pride.

He crawled up after her, drew up her legs, and then parted them. The ropes under the bed protested as he moved over the bed on his knees until he was close enough to swing his root up and penetrate her.

"Don't hurt me, please!" she cried. Her brown eyes widened as she tried to sink in the bedcovers under him. But he had it stuck in her and he aimed to enjoy every minute,

"Aw, hell, it won't hurt you. All you're going to know is a real man had one in you."

She closed her eyes as if to endure him. He pumped harder and harder, at last feeling her sharp needle rubbing on his rod. He smiled to himself at the discovery. Soon she would not lay there like a log, he felt certain as he thrust himself in and out faster.

Her mouth soon began to open and she moaned. Then her chin rose and she cried out aloud, "Oh, no!"

Too late. He smirked to himself. Uncontrolled contractions began to surge inside her, and her legs wrapped around his ample body as she spread them to accept more of him. *Yes, I knew you'd like it,* he said to himself, and launched himself still deeper. Then he knew his time had come and went as deep as he could, the final flush leaving him lightheaded as he gripped her fleshy butt in both hands and sought the very bottom of her well.

She fainted with a deep cry, and he felt the warm rush of her fluids rush over his privates. Not Julia, but not bad. In San Francisco they had prettier women. Someday he would be rich and go there and screw all of them.

Good-bye, señora, sleep good. I wish I could stay for more. He waddled his way off the bed and wiped himself off on the bedclothes. Then, after redoing his pants, he hitched up his gunbelt and started for the door. Time to get riding and minding the old man's business.

Outside at the hitch rack, he checked the cinch and then swung up, settling the black down by jerking hard on the bit. He could see dust from the cattle on the horizon. His men had not gone far without him. With a wary eye he looked about the ranch. At the sight of someone peeking at him, he reached for his gun, only to be relieved to see a small boy peering at him from the corner of a shed. The child quickly ducked out of sight. Maybe a boy of five years old. *Don't worry, I didn't hurt her. Your mother was a good lay. She may be a widow today, but she will quickly find some new man to replace your dead father. The fool should never have gotten in the way of all those bullets— dumb man.*

"How many we get?" he asked Billy Dale when he joined him and the cattle.

"Maybe fifty good ones, some old cows."

"Damn, the old man wants fat cattle. He can't sell these old hides. Cut them skinny ones out and we'll go back for more. There must be more good ones than this."

"But what if the *federales* come?" Billy Dale asked.

"Screw them! We need cattle."

"That's dangerous, going over the same ground."

"All them Mexicans back there are dead. They can't defend shit!"

"I don't like it."

"You and the kid take the good ones to the old man. I'll take Raul, McKelvey, Vaught, and Perkins and get more."

"Damn!" Billy Dale shook his head in disapproval. "I'll go too."

"Fine. You just remember if we take the old man a bunch of cully bone piles, we'll all hear about it." He booted the black up to the others.

"You, you, and you all come with me. Kid, you stay here. You come too, Perkins. We're going back and get the rest of the good cattle."

"That'll take all day," Vaught complained.

"Never mind how long it takes. The old man wants cattle that he can sell to the butcher up there. Half them bony hides we took back there wouldn't make a good shoe."

The cowboys turned and rode with him, leaving the kid trailing the herd. He could see none of the lazy bunch was happy with his orders. Too damn bad. He knew the old man. He'd have a fit if they drove those skinny cows in for beef.

"Come on, daylight's burning." Besides, he might roust out that woman again and use her; no saying he couldn't do it twice to the same one. He almost laughed out loud at the notion of the big bed and the ample-breasted rancher's widow and the passion he had unleashed in her.

They rode past the home place without a sign of any life. Then he sent them all off in different directions to comb the brush for more cattle. She and the boy were somewhere around. No time for that now. He needed more beef or the old man would be hard to live with. For himself, he took the canyon that threaded out of the hills behind the ranch house.

He found several fat heifers and some two-year-old steers grazing in the canyon, but no older steer stock. After a few hours of searching the brush with only limited success, he wondered if the rancher had gotten word that they were coming and had driven the rest deeper in the mountains. Disappointed, Brocius came down the canyon with what he'd gathered, swinging his reata and punching the two dozen or so head before him.

Some woman was screaming, and he frowned. Had one of the punchers found her? Her shriek made the hair stand up on his neck. Hell, what was the man doing to her? With a grim expression, he spurred the black past the cattle and down the draw. Something was bad wrong.

His Colt in his hand, he stepped down at the hitch rail. He was careful to search around in case it was a trap as he reached the porch in long strides. The shrieks were coming from inside. He stepped over the threshold and stopped in his tracks as she turned with her face contorted with pain and anger. Rivers of tears ran off her olive face as she glared at him.

"What the hell is wrong with you?" he asked, and crossed over to look past her at the naked body of the boy on the bed.

"Not enough you shoot my husband and rape me! But you dirty bastards kill my baby!" she shouted, and pointed at the child's corpse.

"Who did it?" What the hell had happened to him? What did she mean? The last time he'd seen him, why, that boy had been fine.

"Some dirty bastard!" She began to beat on his chest with her fists.

He struggled to grasp her wrists. Damn, he couldn't understand who would do such a terrible thing. At last, he managed to stop her attack. She wilted and he released her hands, still confused about the boy's death. Maybe he'd died of—

"You look what someone did to my poor Benito besides murder him!" She bent over and spread his small buttocks apart, and Brocius saw the blood and damage. Unable to look at the gaping wound, he turned away and forced down a knot in his throat. What kind of a fiend would hurt a child like that? Damn, that was a bad thing. *Some dirty bastard* . . . He rushed outside and puked, using the hitch rack to support himself. Tears burned his eyes as he recalled the innocent boy watching him ride off. Violently sick to his stomach, he grasped the rail to steady himself, and afterward he tried to spit out the sulphurous taste in his mouth.

9

He rode the bay pony, and Mrs. McCoy rode a small mustang beside him. They entered the small border village of Nogales under the dark-eyed scrutiny of dusty brown urchins who stopped their noisy play to peer in some awe at them. Perhaps a few had never seen a white woman riding a saddle horse. The walnut trees that gave the town its name grew along the Santa Cruz, where women washed clothes, beating the dirt out with rocks. Small adobe hovels clung to the hillsides above the one-street business district, with a set of wooden sheds to mark the international boundary in the center of town. Behind Slocum and the woman crept the wagons in a long line as whips cracked and wooden axle carts screamed in protest. They would rest on the river north of town once they cleared customs. One more time they had escaped the clutches of the rainless desert. Plenty of grass for the horses and oxen carpeted the hills at this place. The Santa Cruz River would have clean water to drink at last, and there were several holes deep enough to bathe in for some of the men.

Mrs. McCoy's violet blue eyes were puffy from crying, but her back was straight as she rode beside him. To protect her face from the sun, she wore a wide-brim straw hat with a tie-down under her delicate oval chin. Such thin lips, he mused as he took the opportunity to study her while she looked away and nodded to an old man who'd stopped and

51

removed his tattered sombrero out of respect for her. With her small breasts and slender waist, she looked more like a young girl than a woman in her mid-twenties.

"So I will sleep in a hotel tonight?" she asked, turning in the saddle.

"Yes, that's the best place. The men drink a lot at stops like this. I think you'd be much safer in a hotel room."

"They all act very polite to me." Her violet eyes had a way of peering deeply at him when she set her matted thick lashes.

"They haven't been drunk yet."

"You know, sometimes I think I have a father in you rather than a protector."

"Whatever," he said, and twisted in the saddle to look back at the train. Tomas was at the head of the line of wagons as they came on like a great serpent. Good. He could argue with the customs man for a change. Slocum touched his hat to the border guard, who stood up holding a Springfield rifle as if he intended to stop a large-scale invasion of his homeland.

"You made it back," the guard said.

"Me or her?" Slocum asked, reining up his horse.

"You. Why, we heard that bandits had robbed your train."

"Not our train. I never saw any sign of them," he said with a shrug. "The rumor must be wrong."

"Must be," the man said as he called over his shoulder for someone inside the wooden shed to come out. Tomas, who'd ridden up, had the train's manifest to hand to the official.

Slocum nodded in approval toward Tomas. A broad smile crossed the young man's handsome olive face as he dismounted and they shared a silent confidence—the crossing business was in his hands and he would handle the matter. In the near future, Tomas by himself would be taking these trains back and forth from the Gulf to Tucson for the Don. He was good with the men, intelligent and serious. He would get better with experience. Slocum pushed the bay up beside the woman.

"What is this talk of robbery?" she asked, looking back with a frown.

"They bragged too soon." Slocum thought about getting two separate rooms in the hotel. Then he could stable their horses and find himself some mescal to wash the desert dust from his throat. The toughest portion of the trip was over; in the bar, he would listen for rumors of the Apaches out on the scout in the Santa Cruz Valley between there and Tucson.

"Does he mean the dead outlaws?" she asked, still acting interested in the guard's comment.

Slocum nodded. They'd bragged way too soon.

"Is that the hotel?" she asked as they reined around some drays parked in the road.

"Yes. As frontier places go, the Grand is clean. They change sheets often." He dismounted heavily and rubbed his stubbled mouth. A haircut and shave might not hurt, along with a bath; he undid his cinch to let the bay breathe. Then he stepped around and helped her down. He released her horse's girth too, then hitched them both to the rack.

She removed the straw hat, and then she looked back toward the customs shacks a half block away. A willowy figure in her brown dress, she looked so prim and proper despite the long hot ride. He wondered why she and her husband had ever wandered so far into Sonora's worst desert region. She'd never offered a word about their business, and he hadn't broached the subject. With her husband's death and all, she probably had enough sorrow without being reminded.

"Will Tomas have any trouble?" she asked.

"No, it's all American goods coming back into this country. The agent wants to look important is all. Needs a damn excuse for being here." He looked down the street crowded with parked rigs and then, satisfied everything was all right and held no threat, he took her hand to guide her inside the lobby.

"When one of my men leaves her carpetbags here, send them up to her room," he said in Spanish to the clerk, looking up from signing for the rooms. The swarthy employee agreed, and Slocum paid him.

"The lady will want a bath," he said to the clerk. The man quickly reassured him it would be arranged.

"He will have a maid bring up hot water for a bath and towels shortly," he said to her in English.

"That's very kind of you, thanks."

"In a couple of hours, we can go eat supper together, or I can order some brought to your room." He waited for her reply.

"I should be presentable in that amount of time to go out, sir."

He frowned at the *sir.* "Then we shall have supper together."

"Slocum, if you have other things to do . . ."

"No, I only must see that a camp is made and an adequate guard set up. Apaches sneak in close at times."

"I wish to be no burden to you."

'You aren't, girl," he said, and reset his hat on his head. Something about her made his guts roil, maybe her violet blue eyes, which looked so hard at him. But for now he had to check on Tomas, put up the horses, shave perhaps, and bathe too. Lots to do. They parted, and she went down the hallway to the room beside his.

In the street, he could see that the customs formalities were complete and Tomas was riding up. The wagons were rolling again.

"Got that done?" he asked his *segundo.*

"*Sí.* I will make a camp beside the Santa Cruz."

"Good. Post several guards. The Apaches like to steal things from wagon trains."

"Six men?"

"That's enough. Let the others off, but tell them no matter how bad their heads hurt, we move toward Tucson at dawn."

"*Sí.*"

"Do I need to help you make camp?" he asked.

"No reason," the younger man said, dismissing his concern.

"I will be at the hotel later if you need me."

Tomas made a salute and rode to get ahead of the train again. The noisy carts passing by Slocum made some horses hitched at the rack spook at the sound and strain their reins. He waved to the different drivers as he led the two ponies off to the stables. When the mounts were put up, he would set out to find a fresh shirt, a bath, and the barber.

Five more days and this odyssey would be over. The pay for his efforts was fair and beat many other jobs. Like all such employment, there were big risks, but that was life and what earned him more than cowpuncher wages. He handed the reins to the familiar gray-bearded old man who worked in the stables.

"Grain them and I will be back in the morning for them."

"This time, señor, I saw you ride in with a pretty woman, no?"

"*Sí.* Mrs. McCoy." Everyone found her as attractive as he did, he guessed. "You know her?"

"No, I never saw her before, but she is very pretty." He shook his head as if very impressed with her looks.

"Thanks, amigo," Slocum said, clapping the man on the shoulder and starting back.

He found a new shirt in a dry goods store, and then headed across into Sonora. The combination barbershop and bathhouse was over there. He entered the place. The smell of hair oil was sharp in the air.

"Ah, señor." The man with the plastered-down hair made a bow. "What may I do for you?"

"A shave and haircut, then a bath."

"*Sí.* Sit in this chair and I will cut your hair."

"Good," he said. He shifted the Colt around to his middle and sat down in the new-model barber chair, while the man babbled about the fixture being brought all the way from San Francisco.

"You like my new chair?" he asked after putting Slocum's hat on the wall rack and then spreading a striped sheet over him to keep the hair off.

"Oh, yes." From his seat, he could see the open street and across into the United States side. He settled in.

"You are the *patron* of the wagon train, no?" the man

asked, his scissors snipping off the excess hair above Slocum's ears.

"*Sí.*"

"Did they try to rob you?"

"They tried."

"There is much talk of *banditos* all the time. They are bad down here. We have no law to contain them. You are lucky that they did not kill you, señor."

"You speak of those *banditos* that rode with a bandit leader called Cruz?"

"Ah, they are very bad ones. They rob and rape the poor people and travelers all the time." He paused with his scissors and looked Slocum in the face.

"They're dead."

"Ah, dead. *Sí,* that is good news."

"They are dead, no rumor."

"This bad hombre Cruz . . ." The man lowered his voice. "He has a brother who is in town today. They say he is looking for someone."

"What is this man's name?"

"Diego. Señor, I would warn you that, oh, he is a cutthroat and a bad one."

"How many men ride with him?" Slocum watched a coach pass by the front window with a prim woman dressed in black seated in the back.

"Earlier when I see him, he was alone."

"I shall watch for him."

"I hope your paths do not cross." The man shook his head nervously, and then resumed snipping Slocum's hair.

The haircut complete, the man lathered Slocum's face with a brush and hot soap. Slocum enjoyed the comfort of the chair, and even dozed some in the room's heat. But he did not miss seeing the woman in the brown blouse and skirt in the street who pointed to the barbershop, nor the man under the great sombrero who nodded at her action. It was the same woman from Cruz's camp who had served him tea. The man obviously was Diego.

Slocum moved the barber aside with his arm. He rose from the chair with the hot lather on his face. Behind him the barber sucked in his breath when he realized who was coming across the street.

"Diego!" Slocum shouted from the doorway of the shop.

The short man stopped and blinked as he pushed the sombrero up with his left hand to better see him. The glare of the midday sun was on his face and hurt his vision.

"Which country would you rather die in?" Slocum asked. Diego was not to be dissuaded from his revenge. Slocum could almost predict the words he heard next.

"I have come to kill you, gringo! Where is my brother?"

"He is preparing a place for you in the next world." Perhaps Diego would reconsider—though Slocum never believed it for a moment. The die was cast, someone would die, and Slocum had no plans for his own funeral.

"You killed him?" The man squinted hard against the light.

"Drop that gun that's in your holster slow-like."

"I could never do that."

"Good enough." Slocum never swept the cloth aside to shoot. His first bullet struck the ground and sprayed dust in the man's face. Diego threw up his hands in defense. Screams followed as women in the street rushed for cover. Diego's hands went higher as Slocum strode out to him and jerked his six-gun from his holster and his knife from his sheath.

"Don't you waste no time leaving here," Slocum told the man with a shove. His next shot sprayed dust at the man's fleeing heels. Diego could have passed a running horse as he raced for cover, accompanied by the laughter of the amused onlookers.

Slocum looked up and down the street. For him, the matter was settled. Nothing looked out of place or threatening, so he spun the cylinder until his hammer could rest on an empty chamber. When his gun was holstered, he walked back to the chair. One less *bandito* in town. He sat down in the chair, then not seeing the barber, raised up and looked around. Over to the side, the barber stood trembling, with the razor in his hand.

"Sorry about the hole I made in the sheet." Slocum held

it up to examine the round black hole the bullet had made.

"Oh, no problem, señor."

"You kind of shaky with that thing?" Slocum asked with a frown.

"Oh, señor, I will be fine. I have not seen such a thing before. He will be very angry."

"He is a coward. He will run far. I guess I should have killed him. The world won't miss him."

"No, no, many would have rejoiced."

"Good. When will the police arrive?"

"Oh, soon, I expect, but they will say nothing."

"Nothing for shooting up the street? Good, let's get this shaving done."

"Oh, *sí.*"

Soon a man in a tan uniform came to the door. The badge and brown belt on his chest signified what he was. He wore a cap with a patent-leather bill.

"Who did the shooting out there a while ago?"

"I did. I figured that outlaw Diego had been in town long enough," Slocum said, sitting up, looking in the mirror with his back to the officer and wiping the traces of soap from his fresh-shaved face on the towel. What did the police captain expect?

"Did you know there is a reward for this man Diego dead or alive?"

"Good. How much is it?"

"A hundred pesos."

"Then I should have held him for you, instead of running him off."

"I must warn you this man has a brother who is very mean."

"A bandit called Cruz?"

"You know him?" The captain's eyes opened in surprise.

"I did, but he's in Hell now."

"You killed him?"

"No, but he's dead."

"Ah, señor, you are improving the entire state of Sonora." The captain grinned and nodded his approval.

"Someone needs to," Slocum said, and waved good-bye

to the officer. Then he followed the barber into the bath-house portion of the shop.

"Oh, yes, and your name, señor?" the captain asked.

"Slocum is good enough."

"No other name?"

"Nope. First and last." He was anxious to get a bath and go find something strong enough to wash the road dust out of his throat. His memory returned and he recalled how he was obligated to take the woman to dinner; with this shooting and all, he had almost forgotten what he'd prom-ised her.

In the copper tub, up to his neck in hot sudsy water, the Colt within easy reach of his right hand, he enjoyed the pleasure of the bath and soaked some of the desert dirt away. He smiled to himself at the vision of Diego running pell-mell up the street. The damn fool. The one thing Slo-cum did regret, he should have sent that barber after some mescal and a cigar.

10

"I'm damn sure it ain't one of our bunch done that," Old Man Clanton said after Brocius finished his tale of the boy's murder.

"I asked all of them. They all denied it, but I never did trust that one-eyed Perkins." Brocius poured himself some more of the old man's whiskey in his cup as he thought about Perkins. He never had liked the man, considering him a sneaky little bastard. Something about Perkins made him uneasy, something besides his useless eye. With the light of a flickering candle reflector on the table between them, Brocius sat on a crate facing Clanton, who sat on the tent's cot.

"Perkins does his share," the old man said as if in deep concentration about the matter. "You two just don't mix good."

"Yeah, but I ain't riding with someone that would bugger a young boy to death like that."

"Yeah, that is nasty even for us," the old man agreed, and then downed some more whiskey.

"I ever catch who did it, I'll send him to Hell."

"Good idea. A man needs some kind of stopping place, I always said." Clanton raised his cup of liquor and they toasted each other. "You done good. This is the best set of cattle we ever rustled out of Sonora."

"We'll drive them to south of Tombstone in three days. You be done with me for a while?"

"I guess if you're so all fired up to get back to that whore. That should be enough for the time being. I think I may be able to sell some more later to the agent up at San Carlos."

"Good. I'm going back to her. It damn sure beats sleeping by yourself."

"One day you won't even care about that stuff."

"Until then I'll do it."

"I guess you will. You drive these cattle up there and I'll take the buckboard, meet you at Stockden's pens in three days. Then you can go back and screw whores and rob stages." The old man chuckled at Brocius's expense, but he never took offense at Clanton's words. He could still be in that damn Texas jail waiting to be strung up, or even hung by now, if it weren't for the old man. That was too damn final to even think about.

"Good enough," Brocius agreed, seeing the temporary end of his cattle-driving days drawing near. He wanted to be back in Julia's little arms and learn all he could about those gold shipments.

"Drink to higher cattle prices!" The old man raised his cup. "I hope you find that bugger too."

"I ever do and I'll treat him like he did that boy." Brocius clicked the rim of his cup to the old man's.

"Be good enough for him."

After finishing his drink, Brocius left the tent and stretched his arms over his head under the moonlight. The cattle acted calm enough out there on the flats. He'd show the old man that he could handle a big job when those gold trains got started coming up into Arizona. He planned to take the richest one. He closed his eyes at the thought of San Francisco and all those naked luscious whores. Then a vision of the poor brown-skinned boy's corpse replaced his thoughts of bare-assed women, and he recalled puking his guts up at the sight of the crime. Damn, he had to find the fiend who did it.

Three days later at Stockden's pens, he waited at a distance for the old man to drive over and pay him off. The other hands had already left, and were driving the remuda back to the old man's Mexico headquarters. He could see their dust rising as he studied the purple bulk of the Huachuca Mountains to the south. Finally he heard the old man say "Giddy up" to his team.

With an effort Brocius pushed up to a standing position, waiting for the bobbing heads of the horses to swing around and come across the grassy ground to where he stood. He'd never liked Matt Stockden. They'd had words and the feeling was mutual, so he usually stayed aside and let the old man close the deal.

"How much you need?" the old man asked, holding some folding money close to his chest.

"All you got."

The old man laughed like a hyena when he had the upper hand, a kind of high-pitched fast chuckle. He'd once heard a hyena in a circus do it the same way.

"Would you take a hundred for your part? Why, Stockden even bragged on them this time."

Brocius wrinkled his nose in the direction of the cattle buyer. Piss on him. How much was Clanton giving him? He'd surely teased about only a hundred. Why, the old man must have made several thousand.

"You'll have it all spent and be broke in two days," Clanton said.

"That's my business."

"I'll hold back two hundred so you have something left."

"Whatever." Brocius shrugged. The old man would do what he pleased anyhow.

"How come you never get mad at me? Jesus, you get mad at anyone else who rags you. You never lose your temper at me." Clanton peered hard with his steel-gray eyes at him.

"I remember waiting for a trial once in Texas. You hadn't come along and got me out, I'd a been hung."

"Damn, that was years ago. Hell, my own flesh-and-blood son Ike gets pissed at me at the drop of his hat. Why, he's my own son and he gets mad all the time at me."

"Can't help it. I was going to swing if you hadn't come along."

"That don't mean you have to keep working for me."

"Course it don't. But I never had a father."

"I know you said your mother was a whore. But we ain't . . ." The old man ran his tongue along his rotten teeth as if considering the matter. "Hell, I may have sired you sometime, but you don't look like none of mine."

"Pay me and we won't have no damn tears shed here."

"Here's two hundred. Don't you go stirring up them damn Earps in Tombstone." He leaned over and handed him the cash. Brocius shoved it down in his pocket without counting it—he trusted him.

"Hell, me and Charlie White's old trail-driving buddies," Brocius said.

"I don't care. Them gawddamn Republican Earps ain't nothing but Yankee trash that want to horn in on our business."

Brocius grinned at him. "You just don't like Yankees."

"By damn, I fought them bastards for four years. I lost my brothers and my uncles in that war. It killed my pappy, and my maw died an idiot crying over her losses. If I ever like a Damn Yankee, it will be a fat chance. Why, I wouldn't climb in bed with the best-looking gal in the world if she was a Yankee, or piss on one that was on fire."

"I'll leave them Earps alone. I seen them in action in Dodge where they ran things." He busied himself tightening his cinch.

"My son Ike keeps harping about them Earps. Like how he's going to run them out on a rail. That's bullshit. Don't mess with them. I told him stay at Gleason or Paradise, keep the hell out of Tombstone and out of their way. They're trouble and they all got them damn U.S. deputy marshal badges. They give them out like they were cow chips to them damn Republicans."

"I heard you."

"Dammit, we got a good thing here. If them Earps don't make some big silver strike, which ain't likely, they'll go on. Hell, we know all them good silver strikes are all claimed. We don't need anyone messing up our good business. Where else are you going to make that kind of money?'' the old man shouted after him.

Brocius shrugged his shoulders. He couldn't do that good holding up stages, that was for sure. For the moment, he'd had enough of the old man's lectures. He'd go to Tombstone and throw himself a good one, then get up in the morning and buy some trinkets for Julia and ride back down to her. He was less than an hour from Tombstone, with a damn long ride back to her place in Mexico. Go to Tombstone—piss on them Earps. Piss on the old man—he didn't know everything either. Besides, Brocius could use a good whore. It had been several days since he'd had that rancher's wife—damn, that made him sick because he remembered that little boy.

Who'd do a thing like that?

In Tombstone, he found a new girl in the Silver Slipper. Francie was her name. He'd made a few lucky passes on the craps table, and piled the money up to kind of impress her. She was swinging on his other arm, trying to get him to go upstairs to her room. He would wink and grin at her and then roll another good one. Hell, he was so hot, he had enough chips on the table he could stuff her crotch full of them and not miss any.

Francie was a short brunette with close-cut hair and a face like a pixie, and she looked good to him. He'd already reached around her and felt her small tits. His kind of woman—he liked the little ones. Things were really going his way. If he won any more money, at this rate he could take six months off and lounge around down in Mexico.

"You won again!" she screamed. The liquor was getting to him. Time to quit this and go upstairs with her. He scooped up the stacks of chips and shoved some inside his shirt. His pockets would never hold all of them.

"You quitting on a win?" the table man asked with a haughty sneer.

Brocius never missed a beat. His ham of a hand grasped the man's fancy lace shirt and he jerked the gambler off his feet and across the table until their faces were inches apart.

"You want to die on a losing one?" he demanded.

"No," the man rasped.

"Then shut your smart mouth up."

He shoved him back. The man crumpled on the floor beneath the table and a silence settled on the noisy room as everyone backed away. Brocius shook his head to clear it. He'd been hitting the liquor pretty hard since he got there and it was telling on him.

The table man stood up with effort and rubbed his face where he had hit the table. Then the smiling owner, Ivor Norton, stepped in.

"You going with Francie, Brocius?" Ivor asked.

"Damn right I am," he said, handing her a double handful of twenty-dollar chips. "Cash the rest in for me, Ivor. I'll be back."

"Wait, I'll give you a receipt."

"You might cheat your mother, Ivor, but you won't dare cheat on me. Besides, all these fellas are going to watch you count it." He twisted his big frame around to go with her as the tense laughter over his words spread through the throng of people, who parted to give him room to go through them.

"Ivor, buy the house a round on me," he said, and exchanged a glare at the dealer he'd shaken up. If that bastard said a word, he'd cut his throat in a flash. Francie dragged him to the stairs as a cheer went up for Brocius's generosity. He waved his hat, and then slapped her on the butt with it as they went up the steps.

Damn, he was drunk. In the room upstairs, she worked hard pulling on his shaft to awaken it. When he finally managed to stuff it in her, he lost his place on top of her a couple of times. Once he passed out and nearly crushed her to death under his huge frame. At last, sitting on the edge of the bed, he clasped his bare legs in his hands and looked down between them at his dead stump. No use to try again. He needed to dress and get some fresh air.

"You want me to stay here all night?" she asked him as she wrapped the blue duster around herself to cover her nakedness. She had tried her best to arouse him. He was too damn drunk to get it up hard enough to stay inside her—damn.

"Naw, you did enough," he said, and pulled on his pants with some effort. "I got too drunk before I came up here. Next time I'll show you."

"Why, Brocius, you're a dandy." She bent over and kissed him on the mouth. "You come to town again, you look for me, honey. I want to see that big root of yours full-bore."

He'd do that. Damn, he was drunk. He had a hard time coming down the stairs, catching himself on the handrail and trying to stop the dizziness. At last, he managed to stagger out the door. Outside on the porch, he used a post to steady himself. The night air was not much help sobering him up.

"You're a dead man, Curly Bill," someone shouted from the shadows across Allen Street. He blinked his eyes and ducked down before the horses at the hitch rail, expecting a bullet to cut the night air.

"I'll get you, Brocius! You sum-bitch!"

On his hands and knees he tried to see through the half-dozen cow pony legs to see who had said it. He rose unsteadily, ducked under the rail, and then fought his way back through the horses with the .44 in his fist. He'd get the bastard. He better have his funeral bills paid. Then a red flash of a gun muzzle cut the night—he heard the crack, and the panicked horses around him tore down the hitch rack. He managed a shot at a running shadow in the alley, dodging loose horses all around him.

"Give me that gun, Brocius—" The revolver in his hand went off and he watched in dreamy dismay as Charlie White staggered backward holding his stomach. What had happened to his old drover pal? Charlie was shot? But how? Why, they'd crossed more rivers together than anyone else—who'd shot his pal? He wished his head would clear. Too drunk—why, he couldn't even think well enough to screw a whore or even find his friend's killer.

Tears spilled down his face. *Dammit, Charlie, you'll be all right.*

11

"The food tasted very good," Mrs. McCoy said as she delicately wiped her hands on the napkin. They were seated at a corner table in the hotel dining room. A flickering candle on the linen tablecloth between them cast a yellowish glow on her smooth face.

"Can I ask a question?" Slocum said as he leaned back in his chair and thought about smoking a small cigar out on the hotel porch later.

"Certainly."

"What were you and your husband doing in that part of Sonora?"

"Roger." She closed her eyes as if pained to even mention his name. "He was going to look for work at the port of Libertad. He'd heard there was a lot of business down there."

"Someone lied to you about that place. It is a poor village with little business." He shook his head to emphasize his words.

"Perhaps, but my husband held a sincere belief that someday we would be very rich. All we needed was an opportunity."

"That's all the rest of us need. Why did he run out on you?"

"He didn't. He only left me there because there was water and he felt I would be safer rather than venturing with him into what looked like uncharted land. He was to ride ahead and when he found the way, come back for me. Then we'd both go on to Libertad." She wet her thin lips with the tip of her red tongue, and he could see her fighting back obvious grief.

"Then Cruz found you while he was gone?"

She closed her eyes and then nodded her head.

"This problem you had today . . . the shooting?" she managed to get out. "It was because of me?"

"No, it was Cruz's brother Diego, another scoundrel. I merely sent him packing. He is a banty rooster, but he still could come back and cause trouble."

"I'm sorry if I caused . . ."

He waved her concern away and straightened up, then leaned across the table. It wasn't her fault. Cruz had been at Cienga to rob the train. Unfortunately, she'd been there too.

"It wasn't you that caused this matter," he said. "Cruz was after much bigger fish. You only happened in his way."

"Do you still intend to take me to Tucson with you?" she asked, sitting up a little taller and straightening her narrow shoulders. He was reminded once again how slender her figure was.

"Unless you have other wishes."

"You are a strange man, Slocum."

"How is that?"

"What do you get out of all this?" Her eyelids narrowed as she looked at him for an answer.

"Nothing, I guess, but the satisfaction of knowing that you are safe wherever you end up. If I had a sister, I'd hope someone would do the same for her."

"It has been a strange four days on the road coming here with you."

"Why is that?"

"I have felt like royalty, the way the men sweep their hats off at me and bring me my horse."

"They don't see many real white women out here."

"I understand why. I wish I had a fortune-teller that could tell me what my life will be like from here on. I thought I knew when—when Roger was alive. Today I am lost in this land of cactus and polite men, without money or any means of support.''

"Don't fear the future. A lady like you will find a good place out here of her own choice.''

"It's hard not to fear it. I'm sorry for keeping you here and whining about my own problems,'' she said, and looked down into her lap.

"No problem at all. I planned to go out on the porch and smoke a cigar if you were ready to go back to your room.''

"May I join you?''

"Certainly.'' He rose and helped her with her chair. She put on a black shawl and led the way from the restaurant.

Outside on the porch, she took a seat upon the long bench against the wall; he ignited a lucifer on a porch post and drew on the cigar. Rich sweet smoke filled his mouth, and he glanced back at her. The prim widow from Kansas seemed so proper on the bench.

"Nice evening,'' he said as a fresh cooling wind swept his face. The cantinas on the other side of the border cast shafts of light on the hitched ponies in the street. Somewhere a trumpet sharply tooted bullfight music, the notes sharp and clear. A soiled dove's unrestrained hilarity rang like the bell on a lead steer, a universal sound of the night in most frontier towns. Then another's shrill laugh carried up to the hotel porch. An image of high-flying dresses and petticoats with lots of kicking legs showing for some prospective customer drew a small smile to Slocum's mouth as he considered the rest of the quiet street and parked rigs.

He drew on the cigar. The red orange glow illuminated his face for a moment. Satisfied the night held no obvious enemies for him, he turned to face her and rest his back against the post.

"You make this same trip all the time?'' she asked with her legs crossed and her button-up shoe exposed. The footwear made a small carefree movement that signaled to him she was impatient despite her calmness.

"No, I've only worked for Don Alvares for six months. Sometimes he has gold ore shipments from Mexico that he sends to Silver City, New Mexico, to the smelter."

"It must be exciting."

"We've had more things happen this trip than any of the others I've been on."

"I see. But still, this Don Alvares, he expects trouble and that's why you have work."

"Yes, the border bandits on both sides are thick as bees in the bluebonnets."

"Thick as bees." She chuckled, amused at his words.

"There are Apaches too."

"Oh, I forget that. Aren't they being guarded?"

"They aren't all on reservations. There are bands of them who pillage and rob as bad as the bandits."

"Can I thank you again for the very civilized meal tonight and all you've done for me?" She rose to her feet. "It is getting late and I want to be ready when you are in the morning. I overheard you tell Tomas that we will leave at sunup."

"You can take the stage to Tucson if you like."

"I am . . ." She curled her lower lip under her even white teeth.

"I have money for your ticket, and you can stay at the Congress Hotel until I get there. It is a respectable place."

"I can ride a horse and save you the money."

"It will take us five long days to get this train to Tucson. I would feel much better if you took the stage."

"I couldn't simply take your money for all that expense." She shook her head in dismay at the notion.

"Mrs. McCoy, please do it my way?"

"All right. Did you know that shaved and all cleaned up, you make a very handsome businessman?" She stood on her toes and kissed him on the cheek. It was more a peck than anything else, but it made him nod and grin.

"The stage leaves at eight A.M. I'll bring your ticket and the money you will need up to your room in a few minutes."

"Certainly, and thanks, Slocum."

He watched her swishing walk as she went into the yellow lighted doorway and disappeared inside the lobby. Another last drag and he tossed his cigar in a large red arc out into the street. *Some woman.* He went to the stage office down the street, purchased the ticket for her from the clerk, then took twenty dollars from his wallet and stuffed it in the same envelope. That should get her by until he arrived.

He rapped on her door.

"One moment," she said. And he waited patiently, thinking about all the drunk drivers who would be problems for him and Tomas in the morning.

When she cracked the door for him, she wore only a blanket for a gown and acted uncomfortable. Partially shielded behind the door and acting very nervous, she looked about to bolt away.

"As you see, I am indisposed," she said.

"That's no problem. I only wanted to give you your ticket and the money. Here, I'll be there in five days. The Congress is the most . . ."

"Most respectable?" She took the envelope and clutched the blanket shut with one hand, but despite her modesty, her white legs were exposed from the knees down.

"Yes, ma'am. Good night." He removed his hat for her.

"Yes, and thank you, Slocum. I don't know how I'll ever repay you. Have a safe trip." She closed the door. He drew a deep breath, replaced his Stetson, and then shut his eyes. Better get some rest himself. He'd damn sure have hell in the morning getting everyone going.

12

In the early morning light, the jail bars cast long shadows of stripes on him as Brocius slumped in a pile on the iron bed. His head pounded like a thunderstorm. A helluva fix. He was in jail for a killing he'd never aimed to have happen. Hell, he and Ole Charlie White had swum rivers together going to Kansas on a half-dozen trail drives. Rode for the same outfits, screwed the same whores even in Dodge and Wichita—there was no way he could have killed him, no way. It was an accident. Why, they'd done things together like brothers. He'd never fire a pistol at Charlie.

How in the hell did he get in such a fix? First he'd won big at craps. Then he'd gotten so drunk he couldn't get a hard-on with that little Francie. Then some damn dealer— that was who'd shot at him from across the street. How the hell did all this happen?

"Lawyer here to see you, Brocius," the deputy announced.

Good, maybe a lawyer could make a jury believe the honest-to-gawd truth. Be hard as hell for the old man to break him out of this place. They used the damn county jail for city prisoners. Sheriff Johnny Behan knew the old man. He'd been down to Mexico and they'd visited when he was there. They'd been worried about the damn Earps. One of those Republicans should have been the one that was shot—hell, poor Charlie was a Democrat.

"Brocius?" the man in the brown suit asked. "I'm Remel Harvey. I've been hired to defend you."

"Harvey." He acknowledged the man as he gripped the bars that separated them.

"You know who retained me?" Harvey asked, looking over his gold wire-framed glasses for Brocius's response.

"Yeah. It'll probably cost me an arm and leg. Go ahead."

"They won't consider bail since the charge is murder."

"Murder? Then Charlie died?" He had figured it all along, but the pain of the truth stabbed him in his broad chest.

"Yes, he died a few hours ago."

"I never murdered Charlie White. Why, him and I were this close." He showed the man two crossed fingers. "I wouldn't have let a damn thing happen to him if I could have helped it."

"The man is dead and you have been accused of his murder. Tell me all you recall about the events."

"I was pretty drunk when I came outside the Silver Slipper, but someone across the street shot at me. I saw the flash. Next thing I know Charlie was holding on to my gun barrel. The damn gun went off and I never knew nothing else."

"Hmm, how many witnesses?"

"I have no idea. A couple deputy marshals arrested me. I could have fought them if I'd been aiming to. I come peaceful because I was so upset about Charlie getting hurt." He shook his head in dismay.

"They're having a court hearing in a few hours," the lawyer said, as if considering what to do next. "After that, maybe I can get some character witnesses to testify that you'd be here for your trial and get you out on bail."

"It's going that far?"

"Oh, yes, it is. That Mayor Clum has headlines about it in his paper, saying his paper will buy the necessary hemp to swing you on."

"Already?"

"To listen to him, it sounds like the Earps are about to take over this town."

"Damn."

"What's wrong?" Harvey asked.

"Nothing." The old man would be pissed as hell if his accidental shooting of Charlie put the Earps in power. He'd warned Brocius that that was their plan in the first place.

"I figure one of the Earps will be the new marshal by sundown," Harvey said.

"Shit." Brocius shook his head.

"We better worry about getting you out on bond."

"Do what you can. I don't know any more except I never aimed to shoot him."

"A Chinaman's coming to press your clothes, and a barber's coming to give you a shave and a haircut."

"A shave?" Brocius felt his long whiskers. "Why that?"

"You need to look respectable if I'm going to save you from being hung." Harvey acted exasperated. "The best defense I know is for you to not look like a derelict."

"Then I'll look respectable." He shook his head in disbelief. A shave, a clean suit—man, this was going too far. But Harvey must know his business. That was why the old man had hired him.

"Wear a necktie too."

"A necktie!" My God, the man had lost his mind! Brocius never wore a necktie.

"Yes, I'll send one over. You be all dressed up and ready for that hearing," Harvey warned.

"Yeah, I will be." Be better to be dressed up in a necktie any damn day rather than go to a necktie party. He watched the lawyer hurry to the iron door that separated the cells from the office. The deputy let Harvey out and Brocius was alone again, save for some snoring drunks in the other cells. Be a tough jail to break out of, in the middle of Tombstone and all. His best hope was the lawyer getting him off; he better be good. Murder was a serious charge, and he could sure swing on the gallows if they thought he'd done it on purpose.

In a little while, some French barber who claimed he was some kin to Napoleon cut his hair and then poured on enough stinking rose oil until Brocius choked on its sickening sweet-sharp odor. Then the Frenchman snipped away his beard until it looked liked they'd sheared a black sheep on the floor of his cell. Next the barber got the guard to bring them hot water, and he put blistering towels on Brocius's face. Then he scraped away the rest of his beard, slapped on some alcohol that burned like fire, and looked Brocius in the face.

"Ah, *oui*, you are a clean-shaven man." Then he shouted for the guards to come let him out.

Brocius's face felt like a scalded dog's butt. Now he knew why he never shaved. It was plain stupid to endure such pain and suffering just for some damn judge. This was only the damn hearing. If they didn't get him out on bond, he'd have to endure more of the same kind of torture. He touched his palm to his fiery cheek—damn, the man had burned the whiskers off his face.

"Take off your clothes, hand them out, and Hop Soowie here is going to press your clothes," the guard said.

"What am I going to wear?"

"Your damn underwear, I guess, unless you want it pressed too. Won't make no difference. Ain't a soul in here ain't seen something uglier than your fat ass before."

"Hell of a damn note." He handed the laundryman his vest, then plopped down on the bunk and began to unbutton his shirt.

"Here's a damn broom to sweep up that hair on the floor too. Damn, you're a pain in the ass to keep in jail, Brocius."

"Go suck a lemon." Brocius stripped off his shirt and then his pants. He never wore underwear—they didn't sell the stuff in big enough sizes to fit him. With the cool air on his bare skin, he waddled over and handed the laundryman his clothing. He looked at the broom, and then took it and swept the hair in a pile to one side. Standing bare-ass naked in a damn jail—his life had sure deteriorated!

"Hurry up and get them pants pressed!" he shouted at the Chinese laundry worker. This was plumb embarrassing, standing around naked as a jaybird. If one of those drunks said a word, one word, why, he'd reach through the bars, grab him, and choke him to death.

"Me hurry, hurry!" Then the short Oriental ran out to get another hot iron from the outer office.

Brocius closed his eyes. How long could this last? Forever maybe. They'd probably hang him in his birthday suit. Damn, he'd look like a big gob of snowy white skin hanging there with some black hair on his chest and a face that must be red as a beet from that damn Frenchman's shaving.

The Chinese man handed back his pants and ran for another hot iron. Brocius pulled them up one leg at a time, then shifted his ample privates inside and buttoned the pants up. Relieved to have his ass covered again, he ran his thumbs around the waistband to straighten it under his ample roll of gut. This lawyer Harvey better be glib-tongued.

They locked his hands in irons and then motioned him out of the cell. A big man called Jenkins was the guard who walked him out of the jail. Another deputy marshal that Brocius didn't know made a way for them through the crowd and into the courtroom, which was about to spill over with curious folks.

Too damn many folks—like cedar tinder, all they needed was a match and they'd explode. They could turn in to a lynch mob so fast no one could stop them. He felt cold drops of sweat from his armpits run down his sides. He dried his manacled hands on his pants. That damn necktie the Chinese man had put on him before he left the jail was cutting off his wind. He hated neckties.

Harvey looked him over as he stood inside the railing. Jenkins undid the cuffs and then left him standing there. Why were they all standing? He ran his finger inside his collar. Some of the damn cut hair was itching him.

"Stand still!" Harvey said under his breath.

"County of Cochise, Territory of Arizona—rise for His Honor Judge Walter Henry." The gavel clunked as Judge Henry took his seat and everyone sat down.

"You done any good?" Brocius whispered.

"Some. Be patient," Harvey said, as if anxious to hear the charges. "Sit still, and quit scratching and fidgeting around in the chair."

Damn, what did he expect him to act like? It was his neck on the line, not that scrawny lawyer's chicken neck. Damn, this whole thing was serious, and the cut hair in his collar was driving him insane, and he wasn't suppose to scratch or do anything.

"What are the charges?" the judge asked.

"The Territory of Arizona charges William Brocius alias William Graham did and with malice murder Tombstone's principal marshal, Charles Leroy White, in cold blood this day past."

"May the defendant rise."

Both he and Harvey rose to their feet. He felt a hot iron churning around in his gut as he waited for the judge's words. He was a stern-faced old man with white sideburns. Brocius figured the Devil wouldn't look much better when he got to Hell's gates.

"You have heard the charges, Mr. Brocius. How do you plead?"

"Not guilty, Your Honor."

"You may be seated. I see you are represented by counsel."

"Yes, sir." He started to rise again, but Harvey restrained him.

"This, of course, is only a hearing. If there is sufficient cause to bind the defendant over, then there will be a trial. At this hearing, we shall hear all the information and then decide on the merits of the case. Prosecutor, you may call your first witness."

"Marshal Jeffrey, sir."

"Were you on duty last night, Marshal?" the prosecutor asked after the clerk swore Jeffrey in and the lanky lawman sat down on the witness chair.

"Yes, I was."

"Did you see Marshal White gunned down?"

"I did, sir."

"Can you point to the man in this room that did it?"

Jeffrey pointed his finger at Brocius. The crowd gave a moan, and the judge rapped his gavel for order. It was the reaction of the courtroom that made Brocius's heart sink as he sat in the barrel-back chair wishing he could sink under the table. He'd be lucky if they didn't take the law in their own hands.

"Your witness," the prosecutor said.

"Marshal Jeffrey," Harvey began. "I understand that you were with the deceased before he died last night?"

"I was, sir."

"Was Marshal White coherent enough to talk with you despite his wound and suffering?"

"He was, sir."

"Did he mention the plaintiff here, Mr. Brocius?"

"Yes, he did."

"What exactly did he say to you about Mr. Brocius?"

"He said it wasn't Brocius's fault." Another deep loud sigh came from the courtroom crowd.

"Wasn't Brocius's fault?" Harvey asked.

"That's what he said. Marshal White said him and Curly Bill had worked and ridden together all over. Made some trail drives to Kansas and stood at each other's backs in some scraps. He said that Bill would never have shot him. It was all a misunderstanding and an accident."

"Did you tell my esteemed colleague the prosecutor that story?"

"Yes, I did, sir."

"What did he say?"

"He said that Brocius killed a good man and that he didn't consider it an accident."

"This was Marshal White's deathbed conversation you have related to us here?"

"It was, sir."

"Your Honor, upon the testimony of this lawman that on his deathbed the victim said that the shooting was an accident, I move for dismissal of the charge."

"I object, Your Honor!" the prosecutor shouted.

"Objection overruled." Henry rapped the gavel for order in the noisy room. "I am dismissing the charge of murder against the defendant William Brocius. This hearing is closed."

"All rise," the bailiff shouted, and Brocius did so with some effort. Tears ran freely down his face as he stood in shock and disbelief. He was a free man.

13

The bloated corpse of a burro lay in the street. The annoying buzz of a mass of blowflies filled the air. Half-a-dozen redheaded vultures feasted upon it; they barely hopped aside for Slocum's horse to pass. The city of Tucson paid no employees to clean the streets, so dead animals were decimated by scavengers in the form of cur dogs, buzzards, ravens, and insects.

Slocum dismounted before the Congress Hotel in the brilliant noonday sun. Would she be there? After undoing his cinch, he hitched the reins to the rack and then climbed the stone stairs. A three-story building of cut rock, the stately Congress rose above the adobe hovels that lined the dirt streets with chuckholes full of slop thrown out the front doors by the residents.

"Mrs. McCoy?" he asked the well-dressed clerk at the desk in the lobby.

"Ah, yes, sir." The clerk checked the register. "Room 310. On the third floor, sir."

"Thank you."

Slocum looked at the giant crystal chandelier that hung over the inlaid tile floor, from the second-story ceiling in the center of the lobby. Then the wide mahogany stairs beckoned him. No wonder it cost five dollars a night to stay in this place. They'd spared nothing.

He rapped on the door, and she opened it blinking her eyes.

'Oh, Slocum, come in.''

"You look rested some." He removed his hat.

"I was napping, I fear, on the bed," she said, holding out a straight-back chair for him to sit upon.

"Good, then you have rested."

"Oh, yes, quite well, thanks to you." She wore her blue dress. It had no doubt been laundered and repaired since he had seen it in disarray the first time at Cienga. The top few buttons were undone, and he could see the flat bones of her chest.

"I came by to see if we could go out and eat supper together this evening," he said, turning the hat around in his hands.

"That would be nice. I accept. The wagon train is coming?"

"Not a problem since we left Nogales. They will arrive at the yard late this evening. Wheels only go so fast."

"What will you do next?" she asked, sitting on the bed.

"Whatever Don Alvares has for me to do. Why?" He looked at the sweat stains that rimmed the hatband of his Stetson.

"I merely wondered." She shrugged and held her hands tightly clasped in her lap.

"I have some time off coming and we'll find you a place." With his hat, he made a sweeping motion.

"Good. This expensive hotel is overpriced." She narrowed her eyes as if she did not approve.

"Have you met any men?" he teased, ignoring her concern.

"Was I suppose to?" She frowned with a small smile.

"Your choice."

"There is such a thing as a respectable time for mourning," she said, looking at him for help.

"Not out here. I'm sorry, but I've told you once that life is for the living and all of us must face the future."

"I will look harder, Father."

"Good. I'll be back at seven to take you to supper."

"How should I dress?"

"Nice, like that." He shrugged and rose to his feet. He replaced the hat and smiled at her as she rose and crossed the room. For a long moment he thought about taking her in his arms and kissing her, but something made him hold back.

"Seven?" he said, and turned the doorknob.

"Slocum."

"Yes?" He never turned.

"I'll be ready then," she said, sounding as if she'd left more unsaid between them.

He left the Congress and rode the bay out toward the Alvares ranch. An hour later on the river road, the ripe smell of fresh-stacked alfalfa hay filled the air. Some desert quail gave a *whit-whew* cry as he rode under the great white arch and up the drive to the Alvares residence. The whitewashed two-story building gleamed in the sunshine.

"Ah, Señor Slocum, you are back," the young boy said in greeting as he took the bay horse.

"Saddle me a fresh one, amigo. I will need to ride from here in a few hours."

"I will do it. The Don is in the garden, señor."

He found the small man dressed in his white suit in the shade of an arbor covered in grapevines. He was seated on a bench and sipping a drink.

"Ah, Slocum, you are back?" He rushed over and hugged him. "Everyone is safe, no?"

"We lost a man in Libertad. I never heard what became of him. And we buried some bandits in Cienga."

"Big trouble?" the man asked with a frown.

"No."

"You make it sound easy, my friend. Hah, my darling daughter Juanita comes. Our man Slocum is here," he said to her.

The ripe-figured twenty-year-old came into the garden. Her low-cut blouse emphasized her cleavage, and her eyes were as dark as chunks of coal. Her long flowing raven-black hair was pulled to one side, and she was combing the end near her right breast with her fingers. He removed his hat for her.

"Ah, you have returned safely again, obviously from the

wilds of Sonora,'' she said, and made a curtsy to him. The private wink unseen by her father almost drew a chuckle from Slocum.

"They had trouble with bandits at Cienga," her father said with concern.

"Oh, did you kill them?" she asked Slocum.

"They're dead."

"You must stop being so modest, señor," she said. "You always brush trouble aside like bread crumbs from a table. I am anxious to hear more of your exploits. Father, I came to tell you that Benito Guarrez from the Sierra Madres is coming tonight to see you. We just received word by messenger."

"Good. Are you free this evening?" he asked, turning to Slocum.

"No," Slocum said, and saw the questioning look cross Juanita's olive face. "I have some personal business to complete."

"This man has the mines. I spoke of him before, but no matter. The new law—is something wrong, Juanita?" he asked his daughter, who was staring at them.

"I was concerned that you were sending poor Señor Slocum out without any rest."

"No problem," Don Alvares said, and smiled at his daughter.

She bade them good-bye, turned, and hurried up the pathway through the flowers and plants toward the main house. The swish of her full skirt reminded Slocum of the shapely derriere it contained.

"Ah, Juanita needs a strong man," Alvares said, breaking Slocum's thoughts of the fiery girl. "Maybe someday she will find one, because I doubt that she will ever let one find her."

"She is very attractive. She will find herself a man." He turned back to Alvares. "This man who comes from Mexico?"

"Ah, yes. Guarrez is from the mines in the Sierra Madres that I have invested in. At last I can get some of my money from these ventures and not pay a high tax on the gold and silver. There is a new law that ore from Mexico can be processed in the United States and carries little or no duty at the border. So we now can bring in rich ore and have it processed here.''

''Where will you mill it at?''

''Silver City, they are the best. But the best part, we can take some bars in under this ore and I will soon have my money recovered.''

''So the pack trains will bring in ore with bars under it. Once it's safely in the U.S., you take the bars off and the rest we send to Silver City and have it melted down there.''

''Exactly. Pack trains will be better than wagons or carts. Besides, the Apaches could see wagons or carts coming for miles.''

''So.'' He began to visualize the route up. ''We come up on the east side of the San Bernadino grant, hit that sleepy little border crossing at Naco, then keep to the Penticello Mountains until we reach the open country and the stage line route. There we transfer the bars to a wagon to bring here. Send the rest of the ore on up to Silver City in case they check on you.''

''Yes. We must send some ore to the smelter for appearance's sake.'' Clearly Don Alvares understood that otherwise the border guards would get suspicious. Alvares gestured to the bench opposite his, and both men took seats facing each other.

''I know we will have to test how well they inspect our loads at the border,'' Alvares continued. ''But a time or two of only ore and they will grow weary of such searches. What do you see as problems for that plan?''

''Only Apaches and the Clanton gang.''

''What about a few hundred Mexican *banditos*?''

''Them too. If they ever get word that you're shipping bars, there will be lots of two-legged buzzards coming around.''

''I understand. You should read the paper today. One of that Clanton gang they call 'cowboys' killed the Tombstone marshal. The judge ruled it an accident and they let him go.''

''Who was it?''

"Charlie White was the lawman killed. The killer they let loose was named Curly Bill Brocius."

"I never heard of him." Slocum searched his mind. Brocius. He'd sure recall that name if he'd ever met him. Charlie White had been a Texas drover. Slocum had known him in Kansas. Good man too, a real shame he'd gotten killed. Those Clantons must be running wild in Tombstone right about now.

"One of the Earps is the new marshal," Alvares said.

"They know the law," Slocum said. "Hell, they ran Dodge. From the whorehouses to the gambling, they had a hand in it all. Give them some time, why, they'll own the silver mines down there." He wondered which one was the marshal. He liked Virgil. Wyatt was a bastard.

"Who should go on this first drive from the mines?" Alvares asked.

"I can or Tomas can. He is a good man."

"The first one we will send only ore, so it would be good for Tomas to learn the way," Alvares said. "After that, we will know how thoroughly they look through our packs."

"Good plan." Slocum started to get up.

"Here, before you rush off, let us drink to this windfall."

"I wasn't running away," Slocum said.

"I know. Once I was young. A long time to go to the Gulf and return, no?" He poured some mescal in a glass for Slocum.

"Here's to riches from Mexico!" Alvares raised his glass until the sunlight filtering through the grape leaves shone in the golden amber liquor. "We toast it!"

14

"Didn't I warn your stupid ass not to go to Tombstone!"
The old man's fist pounded the table and the force of his
blow rattled the glassware and plates set out from breakfast.

"Gawdammit, I never intended for Charlie White to get
killed." Brocius didn't even want to discuss the matter with
him. He had slipped into such a black mood since the in-
cident, he could hardly face anyone or even talk about the
matter. On top of that, he sure didn't need another bawling
out from the old man.

"Yeah, and like I warned you, those damn Republicans
moved in and took over! I hope to hell that you're happy,
because all your damn drinking did was put them in power.
Now those worthless Earps are in charge of Tombstone."

Brocius had enough. He turned on his heel and headed
for the door.

"Where in the hell are you going?" Clanton screamed
after him.

"Somewhere I don't have to listen to your harping!" He
took his hat from the peg and slapped it on his head. In a
black rage he burst outside and ignored everyone as he
made for the corrals.

"You want your horse, señor?" the boy asked, and Brocius shoved him out of the way. He had no time for that
worthless sniffling little bastard; he'd saddle his own horse.
In a furious jerk, he pulled his saddle from the rail and

stormed off into the corral, scattering horses, to reach the snorty black.

"Whoa, damn you!" he cursed, and stepped this way and that until he cornered the gelding and the black gave up. Then he piled his saddle on the ground, slipped the bridle in the horse's mouth, slapped on the blankets, then the rig, and cinched it down. His jaw was set so tight his molars ached as he led the black to the gate blinded by fury.

The wide-eyed youth hurriedly opened it, pushing with both hands to swing it wide enough and fast enough not to raise Brocius's ire, and then he slammed it shut behind him to keep the other mounts from escaping. Stepping in the stirrup, Brocius swung up on the black, pulled down his hat, and rode off to the north. He wanted to get away from Mexico and the old man forever. Damn, his stomach was all messed up. Everything he'd eaten for days had turned sour. He didn't give a damn about anything except escaping this thick cloud of guilt that had engulfed him. One thing for certain, it would take a lot of whiskey to drown that feeling.

At sundown, he reached Galeyville. A good enough place to seek some whiskey and perhaps escape his guilt. Dried lather and salt frosted the black's hair when he dropped from the saddle. At the rack he tied the big horse, then he went inside Murphy's Saloon. He hitched his pants up to his belly and leaned on the bar with an elbow to check the interior of the barroom.

A couple of cardplayers at a nearby table were busy discarding cards; they ignored him. He turned back and pointed to the bartender.

"Give me a bottle and glass."

"You doing all right, Curly Bill?" The man squinted in disbelief at him.

"Hell, yes." For the first time, he looked at himself in the mirror beyond the bar. Damn, he looked a lot younger without the long beard and shoulder-length hair. "I had a shave and haircut," he explained.

"I can see that. It just don't look like you is all. We heard that you were up for murder charges."

"Got that over with," he said sharply enough to cut off the man's questioning. He poured the glass full from the bottle that the barkeep had uncorked for him. Damn, he owed Old Man Clanton for that lawyer Harvey. He'd gone and done it again. Clanton had gotten him out of another close scrape. Hell, he'd owe that old bastard the rest of his life at this rate. The liquor burned the trail dust from his throat. He needed to drink a lot more of the rotgut.

"You been here long?" she asked. Her brown hair was all in curls and she wore a low-cut red dress as she moved in real close to him. He could see the tops of her breasts, and when he looked up, she raised her eyebrows as if to ask if he wanted to see more of them. He didn't act interested. Instead he turned back and took another deep drink of the whiskey. It was powerful stuff and hot as fire, and had taken some of the edge off his anger. At this point, he felt content enough to simply go ahead and get dog drunk.

She moved in closer until her breast was jammed in his arm, her right hand being friendly around his waistband. He looked down as she rubbed her palm hard over the mound in his pants.

"I could cure that," she whispered.

"Yeah?" He stared at the full-faced stranger in the mirror. Damn, he remembered soiled doves doing the same thing to him in a saloon in Wichita a long time ago. Why, the first time one felt him like that he'd nearly pissed in his pants. Jack Moore was seated next to him with some sweet thing in his lap, and the freckle-faced rascal had his arm clear up under her dress, giggling like a damn fool over his discovery of her jewelry box. They'd sure been green about women—hell, they were sixteen years old, going on thirty. Anyone who drove two thousand head of mixed cattle from San Antonio, Texas, to Wichita, Kansas, fought stampedes and Injuns, swam wild rivers, rode out hellacious thunderstorms, and held off rustlers was no longer a boy despite his age.

He'd never forget that night when he lost his innocence on top of a potbellied whore named Sugar.

"Will it be your first time?" Sugar had cooed in his ear

as she nuzzled her mouth to his neck and her hands ran over his chest.

"Yes, ma'am." He swallowed so hard that it hurt his Adam's apple. That night he figured he was the greenest man about women in Wichita.

"Oh, you're in for a real treat." Her hands rubbed the aching manhood encased in his canvas pants. "I can tell that you will be very good. I can tell you are very big." Then she snickered in his ear, and then her wet lips nibbled on his earlobe.

"Come to my room," she said, pulling him to his feet.

His boots were filled with lead as she dragged him through the throngs of smart-mouthed drovers. They chided him, and one mentioned that her cave was big enough for a cattle herd. She threatened the cowboy with her fist. The drunk drew back his face, laughing at the embarrassment he'd caused her.

"If your dick wasn't smaller than a pencil, you wouldn't have such troubles," she said to her antagonist with a sneer. Then she shook her head at Brocius to allay his concerns, and pulled him out through the curtained doors until they were alone in the hallway. Then she pressed herself against him and put his hand on her small breast, and her wet mouth worked his neck. He felt ready to explode. Was she too big for him? In his ignorance he worried about that.

Damn, he recalled how he couldn't get enough once he stuck it in her, and how she kept asking if he was done. Hell, no, he was just getting started. Finally she went to whining that he owed her more money. He assured her that that was no problem but that he sure wasn't finished. At long last he came for the last time and rolled off on his back to catch his breath and dreamily consider his conquest.

"You wasn't no damn cherry!" she shouted at him when he finally let her get up. Naked, she stood straddle-legged, with her hands on her hips and her potbelly sticking out, dotted with a deep navel.

"You wasn't big as a railroad cave either," he said with a grin, and pulled on his pants. That had been some night. Maybe he'd have one like that with this gal.

"So you're Curly Bill?" she asked. "You don't come to Galeyville very often, do you?"

"Once in a while." He looked hard into her green eyes and clutched her hand in his. Then he pressed it to his manhood. Damn her, she'd started it, she could finish it.

"You're hurting my hand," she said with a frown at him as she tried to draw away.

"Then finish what you started," he said as he shoved her hand inside his waistband and then drew her close enough that he smelled her lilac perfume.

"I never—" Her eyes widened and her face flushed as his hand tightened on her butt and pulled her firmly against him. Her curls spilled in his face as her hand flexed in his pants and then closed around his root.

"Now pull on it," he said and hugged her, pressing her stomach even tighter to his hip.

"I am, I am," she hissed, and obeyed his order.

"You got a room here?" he asked as his manhood responded to her steady tugging.

"Yes, down the hall." She swallowed, and her pale face looked even whiter as he continued to keep her right against his body.

"We better go down there and finish this."

"Fine, fine," she agreed. "May I stop?"

"Sure, but you better not try nothing."

"I won't." She eased her hand out and looked around as if trapped when he did not release her. "I promise."

"Here," he said, and slapped a ten-dollar gold piece on the bar for the whiskey. Then he released her, but not before he gave her a hard enough look to let her know he wanted no foolishness. He'd had damn women before come around and flirt a few drinks out of him and then run off before he had any real pleasure with them. He picked up the change the bartender counted out and stuffed it in his pocket. Holding the bottle by the neck, he threw his other arm around her bare shoulder.

"What do they call you?" he asked as they started for the back.

"Fallon."

"Fallon star, huh?" He laughed aloud at his joke as they

slipped through the curtains. In the privacy of the hallway, he jerked her up and kissed her hard on the mouth, his free hand feeling her right breast, and even pulling it out of the dress so he could inspect the brown nipple. Firm enough for a whore.

"Don't hurt me," she begged.

"Hell, I never hurt one yet. What do you charge for this deal?" he asked as they sashayed down the hall with him holding her close to his side.

"Two dollars?"

"Not enough! I want five bucks worth of you."

"Sure, sure, Curly Bill. That's what they call you?" She closed the door of the small room behind them. The air was stuffy and no breeze stirred the curtain.

"Call me anything you like. Get them clothes off. I feel a long time coming on."

She quickly undressed and then stood before him. He turned her around and studied her ass. Not bad. He pressed himself to her backside, reached around, and felt her breasts. She moved as if he hurt her. He never hurt them. He just liked to feel tits. Tiring of that game, he turned her to face him and reached in his pocket. He showed her a five-dollar bill.

Before her hand could reach for the greenback, he shoved it in his waistband and grinned at her. His hands gripping her shoulders, he forced her to kneel before him.

"Now you can search for it." He took a deep swallow of the whiskey as her fingers undid his fly and then pulled his pants off his hips. He looked down at his stiff mast, and then he smiled at her questioning look.

"Go ahead. You've got the five dollars." He took another swig of whiskey. It would be an interesting afternoon. He hunched toward her as she took him in her mouth. It was hot, wet, and hungry. He tossed his hat aside and then fought off his vest and shirt, until he could look down and watch the beads of sweat run off his full belly and see the top of her scalp. Her head was bobbing back and forth like a woodpecker after a worm. The rasp of her tongue sent bolts of lightning up his spine, and he clutched her head to his flank with his free hand as his butt pumped toward her.

He'd climbed mountains and ridden bucking horses, but nothing matched this. His brain swirled with the whiskey and wild passion. At last, swollen beyond belief and stinging with the fever of her attack, he pulled her up and then motioned her toward the bed. Numbly, she wiped her mouth on the back of her long thin hand and obeyed him. Her eyes glazed, she pushed herself across the mattress on her butt. He toed off his boots with some effort and then shed his pants from his ankles.

He climbed on the bed, admiring her long slender legs, snow-white in the dim light of the room, and he looked hard at the black patch of hair between them. His shaft in hand, he eased himself through her gates and began to hunch his way home as she moaned and tossed her head.

She was all heated up—that was genuine, he decided, pleased with himself as he fought his way deeper. A grin swept his face as her muscles contracted and their sweaty bellies mashed against each other. She raised her butt higher for his delivery, and he went faster.

Twice she fainted, and each time he restored her, bringing her back to the speed and heat of his own fury. Then she collapsed in a rush of warm fluids that washed over him, but still he sought some relief from his rock hardness. Rivers of perspiration ran down her face, pale on the white sheets, as she slowly shook her head in dismay at his still unresolved plight.

Desperate for escape from his turgid discomfort, he finally rolled her over. Moving on top of her, he plunged his shaft into her slick fluids. Bumping his lower belly against her butt and cupping her breasts, he pressed on for some kind of resolution. Then her legs and butt stiffened under him. He cried out as her gates closed on his shaft in a wave of cramps that made her scream out loud. He pushed as deep as he could. Then, with the last of his strength, he clutched her hips to him and sent a fiery stream out his raw manhood. Then he passed out.

"Wake up," she hissed. "You have to leave," she said urgently, shaking him with one hand and holding his shirt in her other one. She wore a thin duster, and he hated that he couldn't look at her naked. He'd take it off her.

"What the hell do I have to get up for?" he asked, unconsciously scratching his scrotum and wincing at the slight touch to his raw tool.

He frowned and raised up to examine it in the candlelight. In his palm, it looked plenty red. Must have worn two inches off it inside her. He pulled her on the bed with him. He wasn't through with her yet. She fought with him and tried to squirm away.

"I can pay some more," he said to try to appease her.

"Oh, gawd, I'm so sore down there I couldn't do a thing for a month." She shook her head and raised up with a toss of her hair. Then she scooted off the bed and frowned at him when she stood up. "You nearly killed me, you know that?"

"That bad?" he asked, throwing his legs over the side of the bed. "I'm a little sore too." Running his fingers through his short oily hair, seated on the edge of the bed, he wondered where he could get something to eat. He felt ready for a big meal.

"Where can we get some food?" he asked.

"Food?" She frowned at him.

"Yeah, it must be past my supper time," he said, and leaned over to peer around the curtain at the dark night outside. He saw nothing but a few beads of light, and then he straightened.

"You've got to leave," she said. "Because my man's coming soon."

"Your man?" He shook his head. Had he heard her wrong?

"Yes, Jake Wallace, and he's jealous and mean."

"Hell, he can wait his turn. Did he ever pay you five dollars?"

"No, but—"

"He can stick it in his ass. You and me need to go put on the feed bag."

"Oh no, Jake would—"

"Girl, we're going somewhere and have us the best dinner this town's got." He rose and pulled his pants on, convinced that like it or not she was going with him. Who was this Jake Wallace anyway?

"Mister, you don't know Jake."

"Put on your best dress." He waved her away to do as he said, and then pulled on his shirt. Damn, she was sure stubborn for a whore. Most would give their eyeteeth to be taken out somewhere to eat, instead of being dragged back to be rutted on by some ungrateful bastard who wouldn't take them anywhere.

"It's a big mistake," she said ruefully. Squirming her butt into the red dress, her apple breasts bobbing with her actions, she drew the garment up.

"Girl, did you forget my name's Curly Bill? If he ain't stupid, he'll smile when he sees us, stick out his hand, and congratulate me on finding you."

"You damn sure don't know Jake Wallace is all I can say." Her wary look at him was followed by a head shake as she sat in the chair to put on her button-up shoes.

"Then I'll meet him."

"Oh, hell, someone will get killed." She never looked up as he reshaped his Stetson, put it on his head, and then drew out the Colt. He spun the cylinder to check it and, satisfied it was loaded, holstered it. Let Jake What's-his-name come on. He better have a coffin picked out if he tried anything.

"Come on," he said, holding out his arm and catching her by the waist to herd her out of the room. She had fluffed her curls some and didn't look half bad.

"Don't walk so fast." She frowned at him. "I'm so damn sore down there, you'd never believe it." She turned away, and he let her set the pace going up the hallway. They pushed into the smoky barroom and she gave a gasp. He moved her aside with his arm.

A beady-eyed hombre standing at the bar glared at them. A small coal-black mustache was on his upper lip. He looked like a dark Frenchman with his hooded eyes and his stiff back.

"You Wallace?" Brocius demanded.

"Who the hell are you?" Wallace looked him over from head to foot as if sizing him up.

"Curly Bill Brocius." Feet apart, he was ready. Let the bastard try something. "Me and Fallon here are going out and eat us some supper. You got some objections?''

"Yeah."

"Then you grab leather and we'll see who takes her out to eat." Brocius dried his hand on the side of his pants.

"Wallace!" the barkeep shouted in warning. "That's Curly Bill. He's one of the cowboys."

"He ain't walking out of here with my girl."

To his left, Brocius could see her huddled as close to the bar as she could and trembling in fear. Her moans of protest and head shaking only reinforced his steel. Let Wallace even twitch, he'd drill him dead. Wallace better back his hand, or Curly Bill was walking out with her.

"I don't want no shooting in here, Bill," the bartender said from a safe distance behind the bar.

"It's up to him." He nodded at Wallace.

"I ain't going up against a gunfighter like you, Brocius," Wallace said, and then turned back to his drink on the bar as if neither Brocius nor Fallon even existed.

Satisfied the confrontation was over, Brocius reached out and captured her by the arm. She shivered under his grasp as he dragged her around the stiff-backed Wallace. Sounding incoherent, she babbled something about "It ain't my fault," and once they were outside the doors, he straightened her up.

"He ain't going to do anything. Now dry up them tears." He used his kerchief to mop her cheeks and then he grinned at her. "There! Now where do we go eat at?"

"At Marge's, I guess." She pointed across the dark street to where the glow of lamps shone on a glass window.

"Good, we'll go over there and eat. You can take your time," he said as he assisted her off the boardwalk and then guided her between the two hitch racks and the horses.

Halfway across the street, he heard the roar behind him. She screamed—a gunshot burst the night air. A bolt of lightning struck his back and propelled him facedown on the dirt and horse shit. Damn, he must have been hit by a cannon.

He couldn't raise up. It must be serious. She was screaming like a banshee, and there were some horses broken loose and running all over hell, and he expected to get stepped on by one of them any second. And then he would die, shot in the back, in Galeyville, over some soiled dove's attention. The bullet hole in his back must be big enough to drive a wagon through.

15

Slocum rapped on the door of her hotel room. He heard her reply, and soon she opened the door with a smile.

"Good evening, sir," she said. She was dressed in an expensive blue dress. The tight bodice was buttoned up the front with small black pearls. He almost laughed aloud thinking of the tales his seagoing friend McCulley told about those beautiful native girls on Pacific islands who dove naked into the ocean.

"Do I please you?" she asked.

"Of course," he said, and took the long thin matching shawl from her and draped it on her shoulders.

"I have nothing black to wear, and you told me that I must get on with my own life." She raised her oval chin a little higher as if stiffening herself for what he expected of her.

"Exactly what you must do."

"However, I wanted you to be pleased," she said with a small smile.

"Why me?" he asked as they went down the carpeted hallway to the head of the stairs.

"Because of all you've done for me, and besides, I have a business proposition for you later."

"Oh, later?" he asked, his interest aroused as they went down the staircase. From his vantage point, he could survey the hats of the many people that were about in the lobby.

96

Some people he could recognize by their headgear. Nothing looked out of the ordinary to him.

The elegant coach waited for them at the curb, and he assisted her inside, catching a hint of the sweet perfume that he had noticed faintly in the room when she had opened the door. When they were seated back in the deep leather with their shoulders touching, he glanced over.

"Comfortable enough?" he asked.

"Of course. I have always wondered what it feels like to be a kept woman. This is the lap of luxury." She took his upper arm and hugged it with both hands. "I am sorry I have not acted more appreciative to you."

"No reason. You've had enough hell for a lifetime the past two weeks. What is the business deal?"

"Oh, it can wait. Where are we going to eat?"

"A small cafe that is very nice."

"What will they serve?" she asked. "I am starving, almost ravenously hungry."

"Good," he said as they went around a corner and the coach leaned, forcing their shoulders to touch. He patted her hands as they held his arm. She would have enough good food this night.

The coach stopped before the soft lamps of the La Paloma Restaurant. He helped her down, paid the driver, and then instructed him to return in two hours for them.

"Oh, yes, sir." With that the coach clicked off into the night, the lamps on the sides jiggling as it went down the rough street.

Several private carriages and elegant rigs with their teams were parked about. The darkness of the night was cut by some light from the high windows of the restaurant and a small street lamp. Several of the drivers loitered about, talking in small groups, as he and she stepped up to the wooden carved door and he used the great knocker to thump on it.

"Ah, Señor Slocum," Robles shouted, drawing the door inward and inviting them inside. The thickset Mexican man took her shawl and his hat as they stood in the rock-floored entrance hall.

"I heard that you had much troubles this time coming

from Libertad, amigo,'' Robles said in a hushed voice. He led them up some steep stairs, and they emerged on the roof under the stars. A cooling breeze swept the day's heat away.

"A few bandits is all," Slocum said.

"Ah, but I have the jaguar's hide you sent me, and a woman who is very good at tanning is working on it."

"You killed a jaguar?" she asked, sounding impressed.

"He left me no choice. We argued over a desert sheep."

"Is this place suitable?" Robles asked, showing them to a deep booth under a shade of palm fronds. Flickering Chinese lanterns hung above them.

"Yes," he said, and helped her in. He was about to go sit on the other side when she indicated the bench beside her. He moved in, then struck a lucifer and lighted the candle lamp on the table.

"What will they feed us?" she asked as Robles disappeared.

"Old goat probably," he said, and watched the twinkle in her eyes as she shook her head in disbelief.

"Perhaps I should have let you sit across from me," she said as if testing him.

"I can still go over there."

"No." She leaned her head over against him and looked up at the dark sky and the dancing lights of lanterns overhead. They could hear an occasional small laugh or almost indistinguishable voice, but aside from waiters, nothing else passed their way. The booth isolated them perfectly.

"Ah, some wine for you, señor, and the lady," Robles said, and offered a small amount in a glass from the bottle for him to test.

He tasted and approved it, so the man half-filled two glasses and left the long green bottle on the table.

"This must be an expensive place to eat," she said, looking around.

"It is a very good place to eat," Slocum said. "Some men come here with their brides-to-be, and others come here with other men's brides. It is a very private place."

"Oh, I can imagine that. The wine is very good," she said after sipping on it.

"I suspect it came from Spain via some crates marked soap that Don Alvares had brought up here."

"Oh, I see. He comes here?"

"Yes, he and Robles are close friends."

Soon their hot soup arrived. It contained turtle from the Gulf and was made very specially for them, according to the waiter. Then came steaming plates of succulent roasted meat, heaped with rice, black beans, red peppers, and other vegetables in a sauce. On the side was a stack of snowy flour tortillas and sweet butter in a bowl.

"How can we eat all this?" she asked in amazement as he refilled her wineglass.

"It will take a very long time," he said, and then he grinned for her.

"It will."

When they could hold no more, the waiter tempted them with sopaipillas and honey. They both moaned, shook their heads, and waved him away. Then alone, they slumped down in the booth and sipped on their wine.

"If you had several thousand dollars, what would you do with it?" she asked, holding her glass up to the light.

"Since I never had that much money and probably will not ever have that much, I can't say. What would *you* do with it?" he asked, swirling the red wine around in the glass.

"Live like this as long as it lasted."

"But neither one of us has that much. How would we get it?"

"A Colonel Lyle Talbot had thousands of gold dollars. He left Texas for Mexico at the very end of the war, and he planned to recruit soldiers for another army to invade the U.S."

"What happened to Talbot?" he asked, looking at the rich wood of the seat back across from them.

"He was killed by bandits after he established himself in Sonora."

"Where did this colonel establish himself?" He reached for the bottle and poured the last of the wine in equal amounts in their glasses. Treasure stories were easy for him to listen to, especially when they came from an attractive woman.

"Libertad," she said.

"Where are his gold dollars?" His fingers toyed with the glass and he tipped it back and forth, studying the level line against the candlelight.

"Buried in the courtyard of his former residence in Libertad."

"You're certain?" He considered the thin wisp of smoke coming from the candle. If there was a thread of truth in her words, even one as slim as the hairline of black smoke spiraling upward, he might one day be a rich man. A light surge of excitement filled his veins and arteries like a second wind. She'd said thousands of dollars in gold. Even hundreds of dollars would be nice.

"I have seen the map," she said in a low firm voice.

"That's why the two of you were going there?" he asked, sizing up why her man had left her alone at Cienga. They'd been in an unknown land, and he'd thought leaving her there would be the safest thing to do. It would have been, until Cruz and his bandits happened along planning to rob Slocum's wagon train.

"Yes. This is no lie," she said.

"Obviously your husband believed in it, or he'd have never taken such a chance bringing you into such a desperately desolate place." Still slumped down in the seat with her beside him, he drank half the remaining wine in his glass. There were many things to consider. Someone might have already found the gold. Or Talbot might have hidden worthless Confederate money instead of gold. He'd seen suitcases of that dug up by eager treasure hunters certain that they were on to millions, and they were—it simply had no value anymore.

"We have to be careful," he said, considering their next move. "Number one, we must not arouse any suspicion. In a month I will go back to Libertad with another wagon train."

"Can I go along?"

"No. That might draw suspicion. You can meet me in Nogales."

"Won't people be suspicious of that?" she asked, still slumped beside him.

"About two lovers meeting?"

"Good idea." She backhanded him lightly on the arm in mock disapproval.

"The coach will be here," he said, and straightened. "We better go back."

"You have no bill?" she asked with concern.

"I paid him with one jaguar skin."

"Oh, you'll make a heckuva partner, Slocum."

They stopped at the entrance for her shawl and his hat. After a personal thanks from Robles, who also hugged her to show his appreciation, they went out into the hot night air. The coach waited. It quickly delivered them to the Congress.

It was a much faster ride than Slocum intended. He walked her inside and up the great staircase to her door.

"Can you find me cheaper quarters than these?" she asked, standing outside the door to her room. "Could I live with some woman you know perhaps? I don't have to live here for a month. Besides, it will use up all your money."

"Good idea. I will find you a place tomorrow."

"Fine, you are a wonderful partner." On her toes, she gave him a dry kiss on the cheek. "I will see you then in the morning?"

"Be packed by mid-morning."

"Oh, good. And Slocum, I can't thank you enough for all you are doing for me."

"Greed is all," he said, and smiled at her.

She unlocked the door, wet her lips with her tongue, then nodded good night and shut it behind her. He shook his head at his luck and went down the hall, took the stairs to the lobby, and walked two blocks to the livery for his horse.

A half moon rose over the Santa Catalinas and Mount Lemon as he rode the river road to the Alvares house. The towering cottonwoods rattled in the gentle cooling night wind as the patches of light and dark shadows blotted the roadway. He crossed under the arch, rode to the corrals, unsaddled his horse, and then washed his hands and face in the tank.

Blinded by the water, he reached for the towel that hung close by and not feeling it, moved another half step to reach for the customary cloth. He opened his eyes and saw Juanita Alvares in the moonlight holding it away from him.

"So you go and drink and lay with the *putas* tonight?" she demanded as he moved to take the towel away from her.

"Hush or your father will hear you," he said, pressing her to the corral rails and taking the towel away from her.

"My father will hear, hmm," she said. "You come home and run away. Am I so ugly now?"

"Juanita, you are the prettiest gal this side of El Paso and maybe further than that, but I told you to marry that Haught boy before I left. He was in love with you and his family had money."

"Pee-yak, I could see he was like a rabbit. Bam, bam, and he would fall off."

He looked around, wondering who else was around to hear their conversation. With the towel in his hands, he hurriedly dried his face and his hands. Finished, he herded her around the stables and down the row, up the stairs to his rooms on the end.

His small rooms were stuffy from being closed up so long. When they entered, he left her by the door to rush about pushing the windows open. The night wind swept his face as he opened the south window to let in the fresh air. Behind him, she lighted a candle on the table, and the flames wavered in the breeze and cast their long shadows on the walls.

She took her blouse off over her head, making a batlike outline on the walls as she swayed her hips back and forth and shook her firm tube breasts at him. He drew a deep sigh, threw his hat on the table, and went to take her in his arms.

"Tell me I am a fool," she said, nestling her face on his chest.

"You are. Someday I must leave here, and you will have nothing to do. Why didn't you marry that Haught boy?" He held her chin in his fingers and glared into her eyes.

"I saw his thing. It was small and I hated the sight of it."

"You're lying."

"No, I saw it when he peed. I was hiding in the loft and saw his tiny thing. My goodness, even a female rabbit would not have wanted it, it was so small." She made a face at him.

"You are shameless," he said, and then he kissed her mouth. Her hungry lips sought him. In a flash, her arms encircled his neck and his hand cupped her firm breast. No sleep tonight.

16

"Hell, Brocius, you can't stay out of trouble," Old Man Clanton whined. "You jump from the damn frying pan into the fire."

"What are you doing here?" It hurt to move. Damn, his whole right side felt on fire. He was all bandaged over, and the soreness ran deep, as if someone had torn off his shoulder blade or something like it. The last thing he recalled, he was crossing the street to the cafe to eat.

"Gawdammit, where's that Jake Wallace?" he shouted. The whole thing suddenly became clear. That damn Wallace had backshot him after he left the saloon.

"Easy, or you'll go to bleeding again. Why, he left town quick as he shot you. They say you had his girl."

"She was just a whore."

"They say you backed him down in front of a crowd."

"They say shit. I paid for her time and any sum-bitch wants a piece of my hide, he can come and get it."

"Wallace did."

"You know where he went?" Sore shoulder or not, he was going to get that backshooting bastard.

"We'll find Wallace. I put out a reward to learn where he is at so when you got well enough you could go settle it with him. Now I came here to get you. I can take you out of here. I've got a buckboard. Some damn crying whore from Naco named Julia wants you back at her place. She ain't got any good sense either. Guess you could cause some more trouble for me down there.''

"I'll accept your ride. Where's my damn pants?''

"The doc said for you to take it easy. Here.'' He handed him his britches. "He said the bullet didn't go that deep or you'd be dead.''

"I recall some of it.''

"He had to go deliver a baby. Left a couple bottles of laudanum for you to take along if you got to hurting too bad.''

"I suppose you paid the bill?''

"Yeah. He said you were broke as usual.''

"Someone must have taken my money then,'' he said, struggling to pull on his pants with one hand. Probably that damn whore got it—hell, he was in no shape to go get it back from her. He'd be lucky to stand the old man's buck-board ride to Naco.

"Here, I'll do that for you,'' the old man said, and stepped in to close his pants and buckle his belt. Straightening, he grinned. "You may get them down if you need to shit, but I doubt you'll ever fasten them.'' Amused, he went off chuckling to himself.

Brocius slung his gunbelt from the chair over his left shoulder and then picked up his hat. He'd have to hear about it all the way back, damn Wallace anyway. In a bad mood and sore, he followed the old man outside, and with some effort climbed up in the buckboard beside him. His weight caused the spring seat to tilt to his side. The old man glanced at him with a frown, then clucked to the horses and slapped them with the lines. His big black horse was saddled and hitched behind. They were off for Mexico.

He was drowsy on the laudanum when they reached her place. It looked good to see the old fallen-down wagon that her chickens used for a perch parked against the side of the jacale. Julia rushed out with her skirts in hand. Her words in Spanish warmed him and put a smile on his face. Home at last. She helped the old man ease him down.

"This way,'' she said, and led them to her place out behind the cantina.

"Can you keep him out of trouble?'' the old man asked

when they had him seated on her bed in the small adobe shack.

"Oh, *sí,* señor."

"Good. Here's some money for his keep. He gets healed in a month or so, I intend to work his butt off for that pay. Meanwhile I'll take his horse to the ranch. He can't use him now anyway."

"*Gracias,* Señor Clanton," she said, and stuck the roll of money down the front of her dress between her small breasts.

"Thanks," Brocius managed as the old man started out the door. Clanton waved to indicate he'd heard him, and left.

"Did you forget where I lived?" she demanded when the old man was gone. "You shot the marshal in Tombstone. Then you go to that outlaw town and get shot yourself. Were you crazy loco?"

"I ain't been myself since Charlie White got himself killed." He caught his breath to lean over to the left side of his butt, then to the right, so she could pull off his pants. "It was bad, girl, very bad. I liked Charlie. Him and I were pals." He shook his head wearily. "I'd never shoot him."

She climbed upon the bed, stood on her knees, and hugged his face to her bosom. "I can see you were very upset, but you are home now. Does it hurt? Your shoulder?"

"Some, but I'll live. Though I'm plumb worn out from the trip is all."

"I know," she said. "You lay down and sleep. Later I will bring you a big supper."

"Better bring me a bottle of whiskey. After that ride with the crazy old man on his buckboard, I figure he shook me all up." He lay back, and she lifted his legs into the bed and covered him. Then she kissed him.

Home at long last, he closed his eyes and swarmed off to sleep.

His recovery came slowly. At first he was cooped up and unable to do much with only one arm, but in a few weeks he began to use the right one again. Stiff and sore, he went out in the arroyo and shot at brown bottles with his gun hand. Another week, he decided, he would be his old self. Maybe he should send word to the old man. No need. Clanton knew everything that went on anyway.

He went and seated himself under the yucca-roofed frame. Busy cleaning his pistol, he looked up when a rider came up the back way. Perhaps one of her customers. He went on working on the disassembled pistol. Examining the cylinder for any traces of residue, he held it up to the light. Then he ran the rag through each chamber a final time.

"Old man sent me by to check on you," Billy Dale said, then dropped heavily from his horse. His spur rowels clinked as he waded over in his bat-wing chaps and took a chair that Brocius motioned him toward.

"Tell him I can ride and shoot."

"Good. We've got to get some more cattle gathered. I'll bring your horse by and get you tomorrow."

"Fine. I'm dying of boredom and getting itchy-footed sitting around here anyway." The .44 reassembled, he carefully loaded each chamber. "You ever heard anything about that Wallace fella shot me?"

"No. He kinda took a long vamoose, I guess."

"I'd like to get him in range of this pistol," he said, slapping his palm with the revolver.

"You out of whiskey?" Billy Dale asked, looking around.

"I ain't had none in a week."

"You swearing off?" Billy Dale looked at him in disbelief.

"Maybe I need to. I shot a good friend and got myself shot while I was drunk."

Billy Dale nodded his head as if he understood. Then he rose to his feet. "See you in the morning."

"Tell the old man I don't need no pampering."

"I will," Billy Dale said, remounted, and waved. He rode south out of town.

The little no-good cheap bastard didn't go in the cantina to buy any whiskey either before he left. All he'd wanted to do was mooch *his*. Brocius would remember that. Why, if he had been in Billy Dale's place, he'd have gone and bought a bottle to share with his laid-up friend. He'd sure remember that.

"What did he want?" Julia asked, her voice filled with dread.

"Oh, I must repay the old man. I go to work tomorrow."

"It is too soon," she said, looking in the direction that Billy Dale had ridden.

"Come sit on my lap," he said with a wave.

She crossed from the doorway. Then, squirming to make a seat on his legs, she combed her fingers through his short hair and looked in his face.

"Are you sure you are ready?"

"Yes. Tell me again of the pack train of ore," he said as his hand slipped up her leg under the dress.

"He says the first time they will only bring high-grade ore and see how the law works. But if the customs man is not too careful looking at their packs, on the next one they will bring bars of gold under the ore."

"When will the first train come?"

"In a week, I think. He says that a man called Alvares in Tucson has some *pistoleros* that he hires to guard his wagon trains who will ride with it."

"Who is Alvares?"

"A rich man who is their partner. He is the moneyman." She smiled as his finger tickled and teased her. Her hands on his neck, she spread her legs apart for his probing. He found her slick gates.

Pistoleros. He had no fear of them. When he made his ambush of the train, he would cut them down like sheep in a cross fire. The picture of shiny yellow bars of gold made him excited. He would be rich. Then he noticed she was nuzzling his neck with her mouth. Too bad he would have to leave her soon and go to Clanton.

At dawn, Billy Dale brought the saddled black. Brocius saw in the first light that his horse needed brushing. He had obviously rolled in the dust, and had trash on his sides and burrs in his fetlocks. When Brocius got to the old man's place, he would kick that Mexican stable boy's butt for not taking better care of his animal. Then a picture of the dead child crossed his mind and he tried to shake it, tightening the cinch and scolding the sidestepping black to be still. A month's rest at the ranch had been good for the pony. He was his old fiery self.

Next he tied on the blanket roll that she brought him. He stopped to give her a deep kiss, then took up the reins and swung on board. With a nod to her, he took off in a jolt. The big horse crow-hopped stiff-legged across through the greasewood until Brocius hauled his head up and brought him back in a short lope. The cool morning air and his long rest had sure put some fire in his mount.

"Let's go," he shouted to Billy Dale, and they were off.

"The old man wants us to meet him on the Fria River this evening."

"Good." He waved his hat at Julia. He'd miss her. The sooner they got this raid over with, the sooner he'd be back. He didn't get in trouble around her. The black started to pitch again as they loped southward toward the purple mountains. Brocius shouted in time to stop him, and the big horse resumed his gallop.

17

He climbed the stairs to the third floor of the Congress Hotel to rap on her door. With expectation written on her face, she ushered him in the room. Her two valises were lined up at the foot of the bed.

"You have a place for me to stay?"

"Yes, Lupe Garcia has a room out near Fort Lowell."

"What is she like?"

"An ample-sized generous woman who cooks good food and smiles a lot." He picked up her bags and gave a confident bob of his head to set aside her concern.

"You know her?" she asked in a small voice.

"Yes. Don't worry, I would not put you in a fleabag rooming house."

"Oh," she sighed, and closed the door after them. "I have been there too."

"They're hard to get used to, aren't they?" he teased as they went down the stairs. "Did you have breakfast?"

"No, but—"

"It is almost noontime."

"I know, but I was afraid you would come for me and I would be gone."

"Let me settle your bill and then we will go out to Lupe's. She'll fix lunch."

"You spoil me, Slocum," she said as he set down the luggage so he could walk over and pay the clerk.

"Good," he said, pausing. "But later this week, I may need to ride down into Mexico and take care of some business for my boss."

"I don't want to interfere."

He shook his head to dismiss her concern. "I just wanted to warn you that you might have to be your own company for a while."

"I'll be fine at this Lupe Garcia's. I didn't expect you to be with me the entire time."

"Good," he said, and left her to cross the lobby.

He paid the hotel bill and then they went out in the hot sun. He had parked the buckboard at the rack. He put her bags in back, then helped her onto the spring seat. She raised her blue parasol to shade her face from the bright sun while he went around, undid the reins, and threaded them over the ponies' backs. Beside her, he clucked to them, and they took off at a long walk.

"This buckboard belongs to my boss," he explained as he drove through the traffic of delivery drays and pack burros laden with water kegs and firewood that crowded the street. An occasional private surrey would go by with fine horses and women in silk dresses ignoring his glance.

"It was nice that he loaned it to you."

"I'll tell him you said so."

"Nothing has changed about our trip to Mexico?" she asked.

"No, the shipment will be coming in about a month. I will take the wagons to Mexico."

"Good," she said with a nod.

"I simply may have to go do some other work out of town is all."

"I understand. If I had anything of value, I would hire you to guard it."

"Good. I'll know where to find work." He reined the horses down to a walk to cross the sandy dry wash.

"Does she live in the desert?" she asked, looking around as the houses grew further apart and the cactus and greasewood filled the land between the scattered houses.

"She lives out by Fort Lowell. Healthier out there. The army moved out there to get the men away from the town.

Plus it is a higher elevation and the water is safer to drink.''

"Did that help?" she asked.

"To get them away from the town?" he asked with a smile. "No, but it was an idea."

"Have you lived here long?"

"No."

"Sorry, I just—"

"Wanted to know?" He glanced over at her and smiled.

"Yes."

"I'm pretty footloose." With the reins he flicked the horses into a trot again.

"I understand."

He drew into his nose the strong creosote smell of the desert. She didn't know or understand his ways or the reasons for them, but he didn't need to tell her anything either. He reined off the road and up the lane. Weeping mesquite trees shaded the sprawling adobe buidings and the palm-covered remadas. Brown-skinned children darted about spreading the word that someone was coming.

Lupe came to the door in a white blouse and brown pleated shirt. Her broad olive shoulders and thick cleavage shone in the sunlight as she came smiling with her arms out for him.

"Slocum!" She hugged him hard to her full body.

"How are you, Lupe?"

"Oh, fine, and who is the lady?" she whispered looking at the prim Mrs. McCoy siting straight-backed on the seat under her parasol.

"Señora McCoy. She is the one I told you about. She needs to board with you for a few weeks. Her husband was killed by Seris Indians in Sonora two weeks ago."

"Oh, my," she said. "Such a shame and she is so young." She hurried over and put out her hand to help Mrs. McCoy down from the seat. "Come, my dear, you must get out of this hot sun. You will soon cook out here in this sun. In the shade we can chatter like monkeys."

"I'm fine." She looked at Slocum for help, but Lupe was not to be put off and herded her toward the main house.

"You will see, I have a special room for my lady guests. You will like it."

He followed and brought the valises. He could see the flag flapping in the breeze at the fort in the distance to the east. Above the cluster of houses that Lupe owned and shared with relatives and others towered the Catalina Mountains, forested with the great saquaros. Mrs. McCoy would be safe here, and in a few weeks he'd put her on the Nogales stage. From there, they could work their way back down to Libertad without drawing interest, and then they could search for the treasure that she sought.

After lunch with the two women, Lupe's daughters, and numerous female cousins, all of whom wanted his attention, he drove back to the Alvares ranch and put up the team.

He noticed Tomas was at the blacksmith shop with some saddle horses. Obviously he was having the smithy Baldor shoe them. Slocum waved to the stable man, then went to the smithy shop.

He and Tomas squatted in the shade outside the shop to talk. The sound of the farrier pounding shoes and the bellows blowing on the coals carried from inside, along with the acrid odor of smoldering coal in the forge drifting on the soft wind.

Slocum planned to ride along and scout for the first pack train of ore. Tomas would be in charge, while Slocum rode ahead to learn what he could about the lay of the land and the problems that might mark the way.

"I will get you past the Penticellos before I ride back here," Slocum offered. "We can watch for any interest in the train. Most robbers don't even want high-grade ore. They ain't got a thing they can do with it. But there damn sure are some greedy ones on both sides of the border."

Tomas nodded, and then he glanced at Juanita as she crossed the yard slapping the leg of her leather skirt with a quirt in her hand. She never even looked at them, busy on her own business.

"She is a hellcat, isn't she?" Tomas said softly.

"You like her?"

"Oh, but I am a poor *pistolero*." Tomas shrugged. "How could I ever impress such a rich man's daughter?"

"She is strong-willed and very spoiled," Slocum said to warn the young man.

"Ah, *sí,* but she is also like a good horse. I like them with spirit."

"Needs to be broken to ride," Slocum mused softly.

"Sí."

"Some horses are never broken."

"Ah, but I would like to try," Tomas said, and busied himself drawing in the dirt with a stick.

"When do we need to leave?" Slocum asked, changing the subject.

"In the morning." Tomas looked undecided. This was his first time as leader of the train, the real one in charge.

"Good. I will be ready." Slocum would cut him no slack.

"You won't tell her what I said?" Tomas asked under his breath with concern. "I do not wish to be a laughing-stock."

"When would I tell her such things?"

Tomas looked off toward the river and shrugged. "But you know much about women."

"No man knows much about women like Juanita Alvares." They both laughed at his words.

Darkness filled the river valley. Slocum planted his boots on the top of the wall that surrounded his porch and leaned back smoking his cigar. The cool air of evening had began to replace the day's heat, and he intended to soak it up. Later he had to get some items together to take with him. Tomas would be ready at first light to ride for Mexico whether Slocum was or not.

He heard the sounds of her thin soles on the stairs with their small scratching of the grit on them. He drew on the cigar and then ran his hand over his face. He should have found a barber to shave it, but the time spent to take Mrs. McCoy out to Lupe's had taken much of the day.

"So you ride in the morning for Mexico?" Juanita asked from the head of the stairs.

"You know so much, why do you come tell me? Are you my new boss?"

"Hmm," she sniffed. "Someone has to keep you straight so you know where to go next." She worked her way along the wall with her back to the night.

"Have a seat."

"I cannot stay. I merely came to see what you were thinking."

"Thinking about what?"

"Oh, you have not found me a new man to marry?"

"I thought perhaps Tomas." She began to pace like a lion behind him.

"Why him?" She stopped and glared at him.

"But he is too handsome for you. You like big men and he is thin."

"You told my father that he is making a good boss." She leaned over and looked into his eyes.

"He is, but you would never—no, no, not Tomas. Besides . . ."

"Besides what?" she demanded.

"Besides, he would never do for you." He waved such a notion away with his hands.

"I could be the judge. His smile is very handsome. I like him, but he is a boy. But I could have him if I wanted him."

"How?"

"I could put a spell on him." She moved his boots down and then sat on his lap. "Like I did you."

"But that might not catch him."

"Oh, yes, it would. He is not steel like you." She jabbed him in the stomach muscles. "He would want to possess what I give him."

Her palm ran down his stubbled face as if testing it. Then she rocked her butt on his legs and flashed her firm cleavage in the starlight for his benefit.

"I would bet, if I wanted him to, he would marry me," she said.

"I'd bet he wouldn't."

"You will see!" She kissed him tenderly on the lips, then stood up and straightened her skirt. "I will go trap him now."

"Good luck," he said, and gave her a wave of his hand as she started to leave. Then he put his boots back up on the wall. Her perfume hung in his nostrils as he listened to her soft footfalls on the steps. Poor Tomas might not get up at dawn either.

From his vest he drew another small cigar. The orange flame of the match blinded him for a second. Then he drew in the sweet smoke. Perhaps he should have better warned the boy that Juanita was a witch too—no, they would be fine together. He drew deep and then exhaled.

18

Gun smoke burned his nose. Three *vaqueros* were still alive in the adobe building and to judge from their return fire, they were going out of this world shooting away. It was supposed to be a simple horse raid. If the cowboys had done what he'd said and ridden in guns blazing, instead of coming in as if they were afraid of their shadows, it would have sent the damn ranch hands fleeing. Seated on his butt behind the wall, Brocius reloaded the Colt, growing angrier by the minute with the *vaqueros'* fierce resistance.

"You reckon that Vaught is around back yet?" Billy Dale asked, sounding impatient, unwilling to stick his head above the wall's edge and fire.

"Who knows where he went. I'm more pissed that damn Perkins isn't out here helping us." Brocius searched around for sight of the one-eyed man.

"Yeah, you sent him to the main house a half hour ago."

"He should have taken all them captive by now. Those damn *vaqueros* left in that adobe intend to die today, don't they? You loaded?" he asked Billy Dale.

"Sure."

"Then let's fire away," Brocious shouted, and rose up slinging lead with both his fists full of blazing Colts. He thumbed back the hammers and fired away, chipping away plaster and hitting the wood framework around the doorway. Enough was enough. He wanted this encounter over with.

His and Billy Dale's shooting silenced the return fire. Brocius stuck the Colt in his left hand into his waistband as he stalked across the open ground, reloading the other Colt as he went. Damn *vaqueros* anyway. His blood boiled at the turn of events. They'd only planned to ride in and steal the saddle horses in the corral. Riding horses were selling at a premium at Tombstone, and the old man wanted a herd of them to peddle.

"Get out here in the sunlight," he shouted to the hovel.

A small haggard-looking man came out holding his arm, his hand bloody from gripping the wound. He tossed his head toward the shack and then shook it. "They are all dead," he said.

"So are you." Brocius fired point-blank into his face. The man's head flew backward. Then he slammed on his back on the ground. Brocius never looked back, heading for the house, the rage inside him making his heart beat so hard he could feel it thump in his chest. No-good bastards anyway. They'd learn better than to resist.

A woman was screaming somewhere. Where in the hell was Perkins? He saw Vaught coming from the corrals as if he was stalking something.

"Where in the hell have you been?" Brocius demanded when the man joined them.

"I thought they were through fighting."

"Dammit, you better get smarter or ride with someone else." Brocius stomped past him. "I'm tired of doing everything. Billy Dale, go get the saddle horses."

"You need me?" Vaught asked.

"Go help him and then the two of you get that bunch of horses gathered. The old man's going to think we're a bunch of dumb kids. Four *vaqueros* with old cap-and-ball pistols and you two act like they were a hundred Apaches."

He didn't care who he made mad. It was like leading a bunch of kids, not experienced outlaws. He reached the front door and blinked at the sight of Perkins with a huge skinning knife in his hand standing over a woman on the bed.

"What the hell are you doing?" Brocius demanded.

"Fixing her," Perkins said, looking back at him with a demonic smile on his thin mouth.

"We ain't got time for that. Get your ass out there and help the others." He wondered for a moment if the blue-eyed man would obey his order. For a long second he held the knife as if considering what he'd do next. *You little bastard, you better sheathe that knife or you're going to die.* Then, as if he'd heard Brocius's words and changed his mind, he stuck the knife in his belt and swept past Brocius talking under his breath.

Brocius stepped over and looked down at the woman holding her bloody hands to her face as she huddled in a fetal position. Beyond screaming, she whimpered in fear and pain. No telling how bad she was cut up. Sick to his stomach at the man's handiwork, he went outside and found his horse hitched to the rack. They were already chousing the horses out of the pens. He mounted the black and headed for the river crossing. The old man should be happy they had close to forty mounts in the bunch.

"They're bringing in over three dozen horses," he said, standing and talking to Clanton on the stream bank. The old man idly dimpled the swirling water with small stones he tossed in.

"Good. You think we can find a couple hundred more?"

"Not down here." For crying out loud, the old man was so damn greedy. They bust their ass stealing a herd and he wants even more.

"Well, it is a damn sight easier to rustle horses down here than in the States."

"There aren't enough broke horses down here to bother with. We've hit all the big places. The others only have a few head of saddle stock."

"In a few weeks I'll need some more cattle."

"Send word."

"I owe you some money," the old man offered.

"I figured *I* owed *you*."

"Naw, you got that paid." Clanton counted out two hundred dollars.

Brocius thanked him and then went for his horse. No

need to complain about the gutless crew. The old man would get wind of it. Didn't matter if he wanted to bunk and feed a madman like Perkins and two lazy gunhands like Billy Dale and Vaught. Brocius swung up on the black and waved good-bye. The sun faded fast over the saw-edged mountain to the west.

He rode back to Naco in the dark, the coyotes keeping him company. Near dawn he dropped off the ridge and toward the dark outline of the jacales and remadas. His horse finally in the corral, he packed his gear on his shoulder walking to her place, the cool predawn wind in his face. He dropped the saddle, bedroll, and rifle on the porch and stretched his broad frame. His arms reached over his head as he yawned. Why, he could sleep for two days.

"Is that you, Billy?" she whispered from the bed when he entered the room.

"It ain't Jefferson Davis." Busy toeing off his boots, he thought about her small subtle body. He pulled the shirt off over his head, then stripped off his pants, and the cool air rushed over his bare skin as he climbed on the mattress.

"Ah, you are back," she gushed as they sought each other on the protesting bed.

The first mule train was coming with ore. Brocius sat out of the morning sunshine on the cantina porch drinking mescal. She had told him all the details the night before. He felt relieved that he was back in time to observe the train's strength and route. From his seat in the shade, he could see the customs shack. The pack train would come through at this point on the border. Then it would head north to the Silver City smelter, right up the San Bernadino Valley. Good. He would trail them carefully. Chances were they would pick a route close to the mountains for secrecy. The valley was too open and they could be vulnerable to an Apache attack.

He intended to track them the entire route. Somewhere he would find the best spot to ambush the first bullion-bearing train. This would not be another fiasco like that foiled stage robbery; he would be ready to take the whole train and leave nothing to chance. He raised the cup to sip the fiery liquor. No mistakes this time. For the next few days he had only to wait and consider how many men he must have. That would depend on the *pistoleros* they hired to guard the train. Armed *peon* drivers were one thing, but hardcase men who lived by their guns died hard too; they were another matter.

So the days passed slowly as he watched and waited, wondering if the agent Phillipe had lied to his Julia. Then, late on the third day, he heard the lead mare's bell. It was music to his ears, and he lifted his glass and in silence toasted the gods for being so generous. The long line of mules impressed him. There were perhaps fifty or more pack animals. A half-dozen men armed with rifles rode in various positions alongside the train. Several drivers were on horseback, and others on foot drove the animals.

A handsome young man on a gray horse looked to be the one in charge. His sombrero rested on his shoulders as he rode up and down the line and lined up the drivers. The sun shone on his raven-black hair. Someone came out of the guard shack and the young man handed him some papers. Papers for ore to be smelted in the U.S., no duty due. How could the commissioner make any money with no taxes on such imports? Brocius sat back in his chair. How closely would they examine the first such train? Close this first time, he figured. The train would be there for a half a day while they looked through it. No need for him to rush. There would be plenty of time to follow them.

19

The serape and dusty sombrero made him look less out of place. In front of the cantina, Slocum dropped heavily out of the saddle and hitched his brown horse. He recognized the big man on the porch, a big-gutted individual drinking from a pottery cup who gave Slocum a curt nod. A hundred names went through Slocum's mind as he went by him and stepped inside the cantina. Then he remembered. William Graham. Where had they met? Dodge or Wichita? Slocum couldn't put it quite straight as he gestured to the bartender. Somewhere they had crossed trails, and it had not been pleasant.

"Two bottles of mescal," Slocum ordered.

"Ah, you are going to drink much today, señor?" the small Mexican behind the bar asked.

"Naw, I'm taking some along with me."

"*Sí*, a good idea, for it is long way to the next town if you ride north, señor."

"I figured so."

Slocum paid the man and then went outside to learn what he could about the big man on the porch and the cause for his presence in this border town. Outside, he never gave a sideways glance to Graham, though he felt the man's glare was upon him the whole distance to the hitch rack.

"I know you, mister?" Graham asked.

"I doubt it," Slocum said, putting the bottle in his saddlebags and not looking toward the man.

"I know you from my cattle-driving days."

"We've all done that."

"No, we met up in those days."

"So?" Slocum looked at him mildly. What was Graham doing in a sleepy place like this anyway?

"You need work?"

"How much does it pay?"

"More than punching cows."

"Must be tough work then." Slocum checked his cinch as if it was of interest to him. Down the street, the restless mules were milling and bawling. Was Graham there to survey the pack train?

"No, it would be easy work for a fella like you."

"I better keep moseying along. I hate this damn desert country." Slocum mounted up and reined the bay around. "What's all them mules carrying that they stopped down here?" He jerked a thumb in their direction.

"Ore."

"Ore?"

"High-grade ore. New law, they can bring it in without paying the duty."

Slocum looked off at the milling and honking mules as if he had never considered the cargo. If the mule train's contents were no secret to the likes of William Graham, then too many people knew their business. Damn, they would certainly need more guards when they brought bullion instead of ore.

"Be lots of stamping, huh?" He turned to look at the man.

"Lots of it," Brocius said. "My name's Curly Bill."

"Good to see you," Slocum said, not offering him his name, and made a salute to the brim of his sombrero with his fingers.

"Hey," Brocius said. "You get to needing some money, drop by. I might have work."

"I might do that." He reined the bay around and set out at a trot for the north and the U.S. Where had he heard of Curly Bill? Damn, was he the one who shot Marshal Charlie White and got off? Slocum had known him as William Graham in Kansas, but now he obviously called himself Curly Bill. Curly Bill Brocius! He was one of the cowboys that rode for Old Man Clanton. Hell, at that rate, everyone knew the mining company's business. They would need to double the number of guards to ever bring the bullion in. Somewhere someone was revealing all their secrets.

After sundown he circled back and entered the camp of the packers. The night guards recognized him with a nod when he rode past them to the picket line. Slocum loosened the girth on the brown pony, and Tomas joined him.

"Did the boarder guards search much?" Slocum asked.

Tomas shook his head. "No. The ore is sharp quartz and they soon tired of going through it when their fingers grew sore."

"Good news. But there is some bad news."

"What?"

"I met a man in town named Curly Bill Brocius. He knew all about the train today and what it carried."

"He works for Old Man Clanton, no?" Tomas frowned at this.

"Yes, he does, and that means there are no secrets about this pack train, my friend."

"How do you think he learned that?"

"Someone told him."

"But who?"

"I am not sure, but they know and you will have to be on your guard the entire way. I will tell Alvares to hire more men to ride with you when he ships the bars."

"I will watch very close."

"Good. It upsets me that he knows so much, but tongues wag too much anyway."

"Where will you go now?" Tomas asked.

"I will head back for Tucson after I eat something. You can surely get the ore to Silver City. Brocius didn't act too interested in your load, but if he knew it contained more than rocks, then I think you'd be fair game."

"Fair game?"

"I mean, he'd try to hold you up. He talked about hiring me someday, like he expected to have work soon."

"They're butchers," Tomas said in disgust. "They rape and rob the poor ranchers all over Sonora."

"Remember that and keep a good guard," Slocum said. The cook handed him a plate of food, and he took himself a seat on a large rock under the mesquite tree. "Thanks, it smells good," he said after the man.

"Ah, *sí*." The cook went off to see about his fires.

The beans and rice were spicy and the chunks of browned goat meat tasty and tender as he chewed them. *Cabrito.* This was a young goat.

"So, what will you tell the Don?" Tomas asked.

"To send more guards on the next train." He looked around, then lowered his voice. "The border guards are not going to dig deep in every pannier of sharp quartz looking for the bars."

"Right. It is too sharp for them," Tomas said amused.

"Be careful. Curly Bill is a backshooter."

"I will. You do the same going to the Gulf."

Slocum agreed with the young man, finished his meal, and then rode out. He wondered how Juanita had entertained Tomas the last night at the ranch. Tomas had never spoken a word about her, so he would have to hear her story of the courtship when he returned to Tucson. He set out under the starlight intending to ride past the Mule Shoes before he undid his bedroll.

The brown horse went lame the next day, but he reached Tombstone in the early evening on the game pony. He turned the horse loose at the edge of town in a wash to wander off and fend for himself. He went up Allen Street carting his saddle and gear on his shoulder.

The gold letters in the window said "Tucson-Tombstone Stage Line." He stepped in the office, dumped his rig on the floor, and went to the desk.

"Any stage leaving tonight?" he asked.

"Couple hours," the clerk under the celluloid visor said looking at the clock on the wall.

"I need a ticket to Tucson."

"Cost ten bucks," the man said, opening the drawer and drawing out a red ticket. He waited for Slocum to produce the money before he handed it to him.

"Two hours?"

"Yep, leaves at eleven o'clock, gets to Tucson a little past five tomorrow afternoon, if there ain't no problems."

"I'm going down to Nellie Cashman's and have supper. My saddle and gear be safe here?"

"Safe as if it were in a bank, I guess."

"Good." Slocum headed out the door and up the busy street. Light from the businesses flooded onto the boardwalk. The clack of roulette wheels carried out to the boardwalk as he hurried for Nellie's, along with a piano's tinkle from one place and the sound of a squeeze box in another saloon. They mixed with the shouts of the miners, drivers, and others who filled the businesses to overflowing until they lined the boardwalk. The loud shrieks of the bar girls filled the night air.

He saw two of the town's lawmen in their long black coats hurry across the street and head west. They reminded him of some of the Earps that he'd seen in Dodge. He crossed the street and went down the half block to Nellie's. Not seeing a familiar face in the crowded restaurant, he ate alone and wondered about Mrs. McCoy up at Lupe's. Perhaps she had met a nice officer—she would make a good officer's wife. She was prim and proper, with a big urge to get ahead. He ate the thick steak, fresh hot bread, and potatoes, a treat after all the Mexican food he'd had on the road.

Later, seated in the stagecoach, he looked back up Allen Street, glad to be leaving the boomtown. He found the other three passengers were drummers also headed for Tucson. The stage roared out of town rocking and bucking as the driver kept the horses at a stiff pace considering it was dark and the coach had only small lamps on the outside. It was no doubt familiar territory for the driver. He cracked the whip and urged the horses on.

They were hardly halfway to Saint David when a series of shots filled the night. The driver reined up the horses and set the brake. Slocum drew his Colt and wondered how he could help the driver.

"Throw out your guns!" someone ordered, and the man seated next to him elbowed him.

"For gawd sakes, man, do as you are told," the drummer hissed.

"Keep your head down," Slocum said under his breath. "How many are there out there?" he wondered as the robber ordered the strongbox thrown down. The driver obeyed. A thud marked its landing beside the door to the coach.

"Get the hell out of here!" the highwayman ordered.

Slocum tried to see who would step up and take the box. No one came, and the driver obviously was ready to leave. Then, as the horses rocked and the coach left, Slocum spotted two men with flour-sack masks standing to the side. Unfamiliar with their looks or dress, he eased the gun down and turned the cylinder around to fall on an empty.

"Sorry, folks, for the inconvenience," the driver shouted. Then he yelled at his horses.

At the next stage stop, word was sent to the authorities. Slocum didn't care if the drummers ignored him or shunned him for drawing his gun, but he'd grown tired of their comments. *"A man could get killed fighting them stage robbers. Why, all of us could have been murdered."*

"I heard you taking their shit," the driver said as fresh horses were hitched. "I appreciate whatever you did to back me. No sense fighting the robbers, though. The law can't seem to stop them."

"If you don't mind, I'll ride up on top with you."

"Climb up. I'd sure enjoy the company."

The ride beside the driver to Benson was uneventful. They changed horses there and were off for the next station. The man talked about his wife in Tucson being upset every time he was robbed. By midday they drew close enough to see the purple shape of the towering Catalinas. Tired from lack of sleep, Slocum rode the last miles in the coach ignoring the drummers' sullen looks.

They arrived in Tucson. He hired a wagon and let the driver deliver him to the ranch. He dismounted, tossed out his gear, paid the driver, and then headed for his rooms.

"That you, Slocum?" Alvares called out.

"Sí."

"How were things with the first train?"

"Good and bad."

"The bad part?"

"Old Man Clanton's bunch knew all about it."

"The ones they call the cowboys? How could that be?"

"This man they call Curly Bill was there watching the train arrive at the border and he told me all about it."

"What will we do?"

"Double the guards. If he knows that much now, then he will know about the gold bars too."

"I will do that. And you came here by wagon?"

"Yes. My horse went lame at Tombstone coming back and I took the stage. I will start the train for Libertad in three days."

"I will pay your expenses for the stage and troubles. It was a good thing that you went and learned so much."

"I told Tomas to be careful and double the guard when you send the gold bars. In Kansas, this Curly Bill robbed a cattle buyer and left him for dead out on the prairie. He is a ruthless man. Somehow he knows about the train and what it contains."

"I will speak to my partners at the mine." Alvares shook his head as if in pain. "There must be an accomplice in their office."

"Perhaps a trick might work to reveal the one who tells them."

"How is that?" Alvares asked.

"Lie about it and then send someone to watch this man Brocius. If he gets information or he gathers up several of the gang, you will perhaps know who told him."

"A good idea. Oh, I have no one of Tomas's caliber to send to Libertad with you."

"If I have to leave the train, Vasquez can bring them up from the border. He is a good man." Slocum felt certain the bearded cook could keep them coming and everything would be in order.

"You know those men better than I do. Slocum, is there anything I can do about this warrant for you?" He frowned with concern.

"No. Too much time has gone by to prove the truth. A very rich man's son was killed. He owns the law there and he pays those men to hound me."

"Such a shame." In the pearly starlight he shook his almost white head. "Could I offer you a drink?"

"No. I'm dirty and tired. I plan to take a bath, get some sleep, and start filling the list to get ready for the wagon drive."

"Maybe they will never find you here," Alvares offered.

"They will find me. They always do." Then it came to him. That was what was different about Brocius. He'd always had a long scraggly beard before, and worn his curly over-length hair down to his shoulders like some mangy part-Percheron horse.

Slocum sighed as he headed for his rooms. All he needed to happen next was for the Abbot brothers to ride up. He checked around the dark yard. No sign of them yet. Thank God.

20

He leaped off his horse and began to run on foot after the fleeing woman. Brocius's breath raged in his lungs as he swore at her. She reached the stream, but he caught her by the arm and dragged her back from the shallow water. Like a hellcat she fought, scratching and kicking him. She was a girl of perhaps eighteen, with a very striking beauty compared to the others that had run off into the brush along the river. Finally, to suppress her fighting, he drew her up in a powerful bear hug and grinned down at her.

"I'm going to have you, like it or lump it." He wrestled her to the ground and ripped off her skirt. The flash of her bare legs kicking only encouraged him.

"You bastard, don't you touch me!" she hissed through her teeth as he held her down with one hand and undid his pants with the other. He almost grinned when her eyes widened at the sight of his exposed manhood, throbbing and ready.

"No!"

"Shut up your yelling, it won't do you no good. My men are busy killing the others. You're lucky. You will live."

She turned her face away as he forced her legs apart and then sought her. Her sharp cry at his rough intrusion was like an eagle's scream. A virgin—he smiled to himself—they were very rare. He lifted her blouse as he used her and watched her firm breasts quiver. He felt them with his rough hand, until at last he finished in a drive that made her moan. Too bad he had a woman or he would take this one back. He could break her spirit.

Out of breath, he rose and pulled up his pants. Not bad. He had to find his horse and catch up with the others. He looked around and saw that the black grazed nearby. He adjusted his privates and then scratched them with his hand deep in his waistband. They had cattle to gather and they needed to meet the old man. He mounted the black and set him in a long walk after the others. Up in the junipers on the hillside, he spotted several head of cattle the boys had missed in their haste. Angry over their neglect, he rode around a bushy tree, and on the ground he spotted the small naked body. He knew by the way it lay that the child was dead.

Not another young boy murdered? He dismounted and turned the toddler over. He saw enough and quickly turned away. The bile rose behind his tongue. Like the other one, this one had been violated too. He remounted and forgot the cattle as he whipped the black into a lope. Someone had killed another innocent boy—the thought made him shudder with disgust. He had only been perhaps a quarter mile away down the stream with the girl when the murder had happened, but the water rushing over the rocks had been loud and the woman had fought and screamed. Who did such cruel things?

"Where's Perkins?" he demanded, riding up beside Billy Dale.

"We ain't seen him," the cowboy answered as he and Vaught fought the cattle into crossing the river again.

Brocius looked back up toward the juniper-clad hills. Where was that one-eyed bastard anyway? Nothing to do but go back and look for him. The old man would be pissed if they left one of the gang unaccounted for. Perkins had a bad habit of disappearing whenever they needed help. His lariat in hand, Brocius went to riding back and forth with the other two, whipping the stubborn cattle to get them into the stream. Exasperated with both the stubborn cattle and the knowledge that there was a child killer in the gang, he slashed away, glancing around to see if there was any pursuit or any sign of Perkins.

"What happened to Perkins?" the old man asked when they drove the cattle into the main herd.

"We ain't sure. We got separated in the junipers and he never rode out."

"Hell, I seen him once driving some steers out of the brush," Vaught said.

"I never left a man behind in my life. You boys leave the cattle here with the herd. I either want his body or him," the old man declared.

"Dammit, he's over four feet tall and past twenty-one; let him find his own way back," Brocius complained. Then, seeing his words fall on deaf ears, he reined the black around and waved the others after him.

"You better *find* him too!" Clanton yelled after them.

"We heard you!" Brocius shouted in return, and spurred the black for the mountain.

The black charged into the stream, throwing water every which way, and then clambered up the bank and loped down the valley. Where was that little bastard Perkins?

The other two riders went left and right. Brocius went up the canyon. Looking high and low as he rode, he saw a pair of boots swinging through the boughs. He reined the horse to a stop, his hand going to his gun butt as he checked all around. Then he dismounted and started up the hill over the flat rock outcropping, his Colt in his hand. He could see the cuffs of the pants. Damn, the man was hung off the ground. The notion made Brocius's stomach roil.

Oh, damn, they'd hung Perkins with a reata. His face had turned blue when he was strangled. Brocius fired his Colt in the air to gather in the others. Then he waded up the hillside to the swinging corpse, drew out his big knife, and used it to reach up and saw the rope in two above the man's head. Who had done it? Some of the Mexicans was all he could think. Then the lariat parted under his blade and Perkins's limp body fell to the ground in a heap.

"What in the hell happened to him?" Vaught demanded, dismounting.

"Someone hung him. Find a horse to put him on."

''He dead?''

''What the hell do you think? Go find his horse.'' Brocius shook his head in disbelief at the man's question.

''What happened?'' Billy Dale asked, looking like he'd swallowed a lemon whole.

''Someone hung Perkins,'' Vaught said, and remounted his horse to go find the dead man's mount.

''Who would have done that?'' Billy Dale skirted around the body as if he didn't know what to do next.

''Damn Mexicans hung him, I guess.'' Brocius tried to recall who he'd last seen with the one-eyed man. ''You see anyone else besides them women that ran off?''

''No, why?''

''How could a couple of pregnant women and a girl have hung him?''

''I don't know. It's a mystery, ain't it?''

''Someone killed a little boy too.''

''A little boy?'' Billy Dale asked.

''It wasn't nice either—I mean, to have to look at.'' He scowled in disgust. ''They hurt him too.''

''Why you telling me all this crazy stuff. Let's get him loaded on a horse and get the hell out of here. I'm feeling spooked by all you're saying.''

''Vaught went looking for his horse.''

''Put him on mine or yours and we'll ride double. They might come back and hang us.''

''Who?'' Brocius demanded.

''Gawdammit, Brocius, whoever hung Perkins.''

''You stay here with the body. I'm going to find them damn women.'' He looked around the juniper-clad hillside. Which way had they gone? He wanted some answers. He dreaded facing the old man and telling him some ghost had hung Perkins. The old man liked the sneaky one-eyed bastard. And all the time Brocius had figured that Perkins had raped the first little boy. Maybe he'd raped both of them. Brocius needed answers. Clanton wouldn't take maybe or I suppose. Brocius needed some hard facts.

''You ain't leaving me with him, are you?'' Billy Dale's voice grew higher-pitched.

'Why not? He's dead and Vaught will be back with his

horse when he finds it. You two load him up and take him back to the ranch. I'm finding them women for some answers."

"Don't leave me here with a damn dead body."

"Shut up. Vaught's coming back as soon as he finds the horse." Damn the crybaby anyway. He booted the black and left the clearing heading east up the bottom. Searching for signs of the women, he headed for where he'd last seen the dead boy.

He found the spot and tracks that led further upstream. He remounted and watched the ground carefully. Footprints of the three women were there where the riders had surprised them washing clothes in the stream a few hours earlier while rustling cattle in the foothills. He wondered if that virgin was with them as he ducked a bough and searched for sight of them.

Then he saw them. They were around a fresh-dug grave, and looked startled at the sight of him. Their eyes wet with tears, they started to run at the sight of him.

"Stop!" he shouted, and fired a shot in the ground close by them.

They obeyed and raised their hands. He dismounted, dropped the reins, and crossed the grass clearing. With terror on their faces, they almost trembled clustered close together.

"I didn't kill that boy," he said, looking them over. "Did you see the one who did it?"

They shook their heads.

"Did you hang my man? The one-eyed one."

They shook their heads.

"Where are your husbands?"

"Arizona, to work in the mines," the heaviest one said, motioning to the north. The middle one cried on the shoulder of the young girl, who acted protective of her.

"Who hung that man?" he demanded.

"We did not hang no one. Someone killed her son Jose. He was a mean person to hurt such a boy as Jose like that."

"I would kill the hombre that did that." He holstered his Colt.

"You should know, you rape innocent girls," the older woman snarled at him in her anger.

They knew nothing. He would have to tell the old man he knew nothing too. Perkins was alive one minute, the next he was dead on the end of a rope. Why had someone hung him? Because he knew too much? Had he seen someone abuse the boy and then paid with his life for the knowledge?

Brocius caught up with the other two riders far downstream. They rode in silence, the corpse tied over the saddle and wrapped in a blanket. Bent over the seat facedown, the stiff body teetered back and forth on the horse.

He wished as he rode that he had a piece of the reata that had hung the man. Maybe it wasn't Perkins's own rope. He pushed the black up and saw that Perkins's saddle had no rope tied on it. Every cowboy had a lariat on his rig. But had the rope that had hung him been his own?

If some Mexicans had jumped him, they would have used his rope to hang him. But if one of the other two men riding with him had roped him around the neck, and then strung him up to make it look like a hanging, they would have used their own ropes. Had he ever noticed the ropes that Vaught and Billy Dale carried? No, he'd seen both men get them out to whip cattle, but he couldn't recall whether they were three- or four-twist reatas. Perkins had been hung with a rawhide rope was all he knew. He rode in close enough to lift the blanket, reach down, and draw the strand of reata from Perkins's neck with a jerk.

"What's the matter?" Vaught asked, turning in the saddle.

"I just covered him up better," Brocius said. The strand held in his left hand beside his leg was more like a quirt. He wondered it Vaught had noticed. They rode across a stream that had gone nearly dry as it approached the valley floor. After a short while, when the others weren't looking, he put the short section inside his shirt.

"I can't believe someone hung Perkins while you were off stuffing yourself in some sweet thing and the rest of them were out chasing cattle," the old man said later as the two of them stood together out in the moonlight. The acacias creaked out in the night, and a half-dozen coyotes moaned at the rising moon.

"They did. Was Perkins a reata man?"

"No, he carried a rope. Why?"

"Was Vaught a reata man?"

"No. Billy Dale carried one, but he couldn't do much at branding with one."

"Let's go find his saddle."

"Why?"

"I figure that whoever killed Perkins did it with their own rope, then took Perkins's twine off his saddle and made a switch."

"You think Billy Dale did that? Hung Perkins?" the old man asked in an exasperated whisper.

"I ain't sure. One of them two buggered a boy a month ago and then again today. I figured he killed Perkins so he wouldn't tell on him. Let's go check Billy Dale's saddle." Brocius led the way to the corral. He knew right where Billy Dale's saddle hung.

"I remember you saying something about a boy being buggered," Clanton said. "You say it happened again today? And whoever did it also hung Perkins?"

"I think so. You got a match?"

"Yeah, here."

Brocius struck it and the light flared. There on Billy Dale's saddle was a reata tied to the swell by the leather strings. Not a new one, but a dusty, dirty, well-used one.

"What now?" the old man asked.

"One of them did it. Because Perkins knew what he did to the boy. I can't prove it is all."

"I'll keep my eyes and ears open." Clanton clapped a hand on Brocius's shoulder. "You really tried, Brocius. You really tried hard."

21

"Yes, I'm excited to be going there at last, and with some-one who knows the way." Mrs. McCoy shook her head and pressed her lips together to regain her composure. "To be quite honest, my poor husband was not the—ah—fron-tiersman type and no doubt that contributed to his—de-mise." In the cool early morning, she and Slocum walked a path through the towering cactus and greasewood beyond the shouts of children and activity around Lupe's com-pound. Above them rose the saguaro-clad foothills of the Catalinas, and off in the chaparral the topknotted quails gave their *whit-whew* calls to each other.

"How's your stay been here?" he asked, seeing the gleam of excitement building in her eyes. Not only did she look rested, but a freshness beamed from her face.

"Oh, very good. Lupe's a very sweet person. She even helped me sew a new riding outfit. She also told me that you stayed with her for six weeks a few years ago when you were wounded."

"She's a good nurse too," he said, recalling his recovery from the bullet in his leg and how close the bounty men had come to finding him there. Only her loyalty and in-genuity had saved him from being captured.

"You need to catch the Nogales stage on Saturday and then go to the hotel when you get there," he explained. "I will meet you at the hotel. That will give me time to get

137

the wagon train there. I'll have a gentle horse along for you to ride and a small tent for your privacy.''

"My upkeep here and at the Congress, the stage fare—I'll owe you so much. What if the colonel's money is gone?''

"I won't abandon you in Libertad if we don't find it,'' he said, laughing out loud.

"What is so funny?'' She frowned at him.

"I have gambled all my life on much worse things than this. Don't worry about the expenses.''

"But I do.''

"I plan on finding his gold.''

"I certainly hope so.''

"Think good thoughts and we'll have a good trip regardless of the outcome. The men think you are some kind of royalty. They enjoy your company.''

"Do they really?''

"Yes, they are unaccustomed to a woman like you going on such an arduous journey. They don't quite understand why, but they take pride in you joining them. I saw that when you came back with us. It was good for their morale.''

"I will try to remain spirited and not act too concerned about the expenses.''

"Do that,'' he said, and drew out the purse of money from inside his vest. "Here's the money for Lupe, the stage fare, and expenses.''

"Here we go again.'' She hefted the small purse in her hand. "I suspect it is much more than I will need.''

"Pay Lupe as generously as she will accept. She never charges enough.''

"I will, and I will be in Nogales on Saturday night, sir.''

"This crossing is going to be very hot. It will be the last one until fall because of the heat. It is a risky time to make such a trip because the water dries up, but we will go prepared.''

"I find myself more tempered to the desert heat all the time.''

"Good. Late June is always a very hot time in the desert with its long days.''

"I am very strong."

He turned and looked at her straight back and erect posture. Yes, she was a strong person. For her to survive the rape of the outlaws and death of her husband, all in such a short span of time, she had to be a very hardy woman.

They stopped on the brink of a deep-cut dry wash. He studied the water-eroded dry sand for a moment. His thoughts turned to the details of the journey. She spoke, but he didn't hear her.

"What?" he asked, blinking at her.

"I've asked so much—you've done so much. Would you simply hold me? Or is that—"

"I'm sorry," he said, and held out his arms to her. "I was concerned about leaving tomorrow and what I would forget."

"I know I am an inconvenience."

"No, I am always on edge before I leave with a train."

She nestled in his arms. He felt her trembling, the stiffness of her body, as he gently hugged her. She huddled in his arms, her hands on his vest front. Then she pushed him away as if to escape, or to get rid of her own fears.

"I'm sorry, Slocum," she said with great effort as she moved out of his arms. Out of breath, she gasped for air. "I wanted—I had hoped to—to be closer to you, to maybe steal some of your confidence even, but I can't." She closed her eyes and then dropped her head.

"Mrs. McCoy . . ."

"Audrey. Please."

"Hey, don't fret over it. You aren't healed yet."

"No, I'm not and I realize that now. Thanks, Slocum," she said, and her hand reached for his as they turned to go back. Her slender fingers closed on his and in silence they walked back to Lupe's. Then they could hear the children shouting and she released him.

The creak of the cart axles, despite generous grease, filled the early morning air. He had four spare saddle horses hitched to the lead wagon's tailgate. One was a fat glass-eyed bald-faced chestnut for Mrs. McCoy to ride. A tent, as he'd promised her, was stored in the cook wagon. He listened as whips popped and men shouted to their teams of oxen. Chains clinked and yokes groaned as the animals began to lumber out of the ranch yard under their loads of cotton bales, sacked corn, and dried beans for the ship.

"Good luck, my amigo," Alvares said.

"Thanks. We may need it." Slocum looked around wondering why Tomas had not returned from Silver City. Perhaps he had ridden his horse back rather than taken a stage. Slocum had hoped to talk with the young man about more guards for the returning pack train; the presence of Brocius there on the border still concerned him.

"You always manage somehow to handle things," Alvares said to dismiss his last-minute worries about the trip.

"See you in a month to six weeks," Slocum said.

"No problem." Alvares waved to him with a smile and the wagons snaked out one after another.

He spurred his gelding down the line to where someone struggled with his team. Somehow, on the first morning on the road, there was always a problem getting going. He would miss Tomas doing all the small things that he had done for him on the past few trips south.

The youth Ernesto, who drove the spare oxen, brought the dozen head out of the corral. With a long switch and a cur dog to heel them, he hurried to bring up the rear. He waved to Slocum and smiled.

Oh, the enthusiasm of youth. The boy of perhaps fifteen was making his first trip to Mexico. Trusted with driving the loose stock and helping Vasquez with the cooking chores, Ernesto would soon learn the ways of the wagon train.

Slocum saw Juanita on the balcony and nodded to her. Perhaps she had found Tomas a match for her furious passion. She had not darkened Slocum's door since the night he had sent her to him. Good. They would make a fine couple. The handsome boy who had never killed anyone before had learned much in the past nine months. Still, he had much to learn if he had to go up against someone as conniving as Brocius with a gold train at stake. Such situations made young men old.

The train made sixteen miles, and then Slocum had them

turn their steers out to graze. They camped at good water on the river. There was ample feed here. Further down in Mexico they would have to supplement the animals' feed with grain. Here the abundant side oats and gramma grass would give the animals plenty of energy until they reached the drier portions in the lower elevations of desert beyond the border.

Later he gave Ernesto a horse to ride and herd from. The boy's face beamed with gratitude when he thanked him. Then Slocum spent the rest of the hot afternoon in the shade, cleaning and oiling the arsenal of Spencer rifles. The .50-calibers were the most reliable repeaters that money could buy. Perhaps when Winchester Arms replaced the brass works on their weapons, he would switch to them. Salesmen for the arms firm had promised a new steel mechanism was being developed that would last forever. Until then he'd use the Spencer.

The way south was uneventful. Many small villages lined the Santa Cruz River. Villagers irrigated their crops with water diverted from the stream. These men wore bandoliers, and even when hoeing in the field they had to be armed against the Apache who preyed upon them. Except for occasional raids on the herd, the bucks with the streaks of black war paint under their eyes hardly ever bothered such a large train. Still, he kept his eyes open and spoke to villagers along the way who might have seen some of the dreaded invaders lurking around.

The days flew by uneventfully, and on Friday evening they reached the border. He posted what he considered a moderate camp guard. The others were free to taste the sin and booze of the border town.

"When will we go on?" Vasquez asked as he worked to build a fire.

"Sunday morning. We need to be there in a week and a half."

"Ah, then I will buy some fat pigs to roast and some goats to eat on the way."

"I want to warn you that Mrs. McCoy is going to join us."

"Ah, a very pretty lady. She will go all the way?"

"Yes, she has unfinished business down there." He felt that would be enough to satisfy the men's curiosity. His cook would spread the word. "When we are on the road, she will need that tent set up for her to sleep in."

"No problem. We shall set it up for her. Such a shame, so young and a widow." Vasquez shook his heavily bearded face.

"Yes," Slocum agreed, and then went to take a bath in the river. He would shave himself too. He felt better now that they had a hundred miles under their wheels with no major problems. He had begun to feel anxious to see her again.

22

He had drunk too much the evening before. Brocius had done that more often since the Perkins hanging. At night in his dreams, he saw the two dead boys' bodies over and over again. Then he would wake up. Cold sweat would run down his face in the darkness as he wondered what jackal had done it—Billy Dale or Vaught? He would throw back the covers, go barefoot out to the edge of the porch, the cool night air washing over his clammy bare skin, and then piss a great arc out into the starlighted yard.

Now, wrapped in a blanket, he sat on a wicker chair in the dark, trying to decide which of the two men had done the savage murders. His temples pounded as he considered the facts over and over again. Somewhere there was a key to this mystery. First he settled all his conscious thoughts on Vaught, the swarthy-faced Texan, as the suspect. A tough cold killer of men, he was wanted in the Lone Star State for five or six shootings. Vaught called them self-defense, but he'd heard others say the self-defense involved bullets in the back.

Billy Dale Spears was hardly an outlaw. He was scared of his own shadow. How could he be the one who'd hung Perkins? Why, he could hardly shoot down a Mexican in a raid. Had Brocius ever seen him with a whore? He tried to recall. They had been to Wichita and Dodge together on cattle drives. Everyone was so roaring drunk in those days.

He could not recall Billy Dale ever bragging about riding some whore to death, the way the others would lie about it time and again on the long ride home.

A shiver ran up his spine making him shake. He pulled the blanket around his ample girth to hold in the heat. A chicken squawked in the night. He looked out the large side window to where Julia's birds roosted each evening on the old fallen-in wagon beside the house. He listened for a varmint like a ringtail cat that might be threatening them. Nothing else stirred.

Dammit, how would he ever find out who'd murdered those boys? There had to be a way. One thing he knew for certain. The place to ambush the pack train was at the canyon spring in the Penticellos. It would be easy to surround their camp and shoot everyone down in a withering cross fire. He had followed the train, and knew it took them two hard days from the border to reach the spring, but it was the only water in the area for miles. The train had no choice but to go there on the second day. After the train left the border, he could take his men up the San Bernadino Valley, get there ahead of it, and set up for the surprise attack.

Why, he could have taken the train by himself when they'd camped there. He had scouted around them undetected from the high points. Still, he would need some good men to be sure of success. This time he would not leave any details to others as in the futile stage robbery attempt. That meant he would have to get cowboys and then share the gold with the old man. This time he would show him he could conduct a raid and come out a winner. A cold chill made him shake in the chair despite the blanket. Who had buggered those little boys?

Each day, he watched the border shack from the porch of the saloon. Many times he saw the skinny Phillipe going and coming from the office of the mining company. The man's job was to have supplies for the mine on hand so the wagons could haul them back on the return trips. Before the ore law was passed, the mule packers only came as far as Naco. Then they loaded on the supplies for the mines and went back.

On Friday evening when Phillipe came to the saloon for

Julia, Brocius would wait at her house for the latest word. No doubt the man kept the books, ran the warehouse, and ordered all the supplies they needed, so he was privy to all the important business information. It was Brocius's pure luck that the skinny bastard liked his Julia.

"What did he say tonight?" he asked when she returned from work that Friday.

"They are thinking soon they will try to get some bullion by the border guards."

"Were they not pleased how smooth the other train went to Silver City?"

"He says they are afraid someone is telling the bandits all their plans. So they will have a decoy train to see if the bandits will rob it."

"Does he know the right one?" He gathered her in his arms and put her on his lap.

"Oh, *sí*, it will come second."

"Good. When is the decoy coming?"

"In a few days. They wait for the head *pistolero* to come back from Tucson to take it."

"What is his name?" He ran his hand up the inside of her leg. The smoothness of her silky skin contrasted with his calloused palm.

"He did not say. No, I think he calls him Tomas." She framed his stubbled face with her hands and then she kissed him on the mouth. She stank of cigar smoke and lavender perfume. "I am worried it is a trap for you."

"The decoy train?" His hand reached under her dress and sliced her legs apart.

"Yes. What if they would kill you?" she asked.

"Ha, those dumb Mexicans couldn't kill me."

"I hope not," she said, and buried her face in his shirt-front as he probed her with his index finger.

He rose early the next morning and left her sleeping. The last of the tequila shone like gold in the sunlight when he held the bottle up and finished it. Then he ate some cold beans wrapped in dry tortillas. Finished eating, he took his saddle to the corral. He quickly loaded it on the black and set out for the old man's.

At mid-morning he found the cook in the kitchen and ate some cold bacon and biscuits. The old man was gone to check on some cattle they were rebranding. So he lounged on the porch, ate, and waited.

About noon, Clanton returned on horseback and came from the corral with a limp. Brocius had never noticed him being that crippled before.

"You hurt your leg?"

"I hurt all over," Clanton said, and lowered himself to the bench. "You out of money already?"

"No. Did you ever figure who killed them two boys?"

"And Perkins?"

"Yeah."

"Hell, no. That didn't bring you over here." With a pained face, the old man lifted his right leg and put it down closer to his other one.

"What's wrong with it?"

"Rheumatism, I guess. What do you need?"

"They're going to bring a gold train out of the Madres. I know when and where."

"How much gold?"

"Plenty. They got a new law that you can bring in ore to be smeltered and not pay a tariff. These operators aim to sneak in real gold bars under the ore."

"How many guards will there be?"

"Maybe a dozen, but I've got the perfect place to ambush them."

"Like the stage robbery?" The old man chuckled to himself holding his fist to his mouth. His hilarity finally set off coughing, until he spat out phlegm and turned pale wiping his mouth on his shirtsleeve.

"Don't laugh. I know this plan will work."

"How many men do you need?" Clanton managed to ask.

"Eight."

"All right, what do I get?"

"A quarter share."

"You pay the boys?"

"Sure."

"When?"

"I will send word. We'll need a couple of spare pack-horses. We may kill some of their mules in the cross fire."

"You have studied this." Clanton rubbed his lips on the side of his hand as if considering the matter. "All right, you send the word and I'll send them and the packhorses to you."

"I don't want any of them to know a thing about it until we get there."

"Good idea. Then they can't get greedy beforehand. How much gold do you figure is going to come through under the ore?"

"I think quite a lot."

"Good, I can always use it." He clapped Brocius on the knee. "I always figured there was a brain in that thick head of yours. You pull this off and I'll know for certain there is."

He ate lunch with the old man, the two of them alone at the big table. The room echoed when they set down their silverware or even made small talk.

"Them Earps are after Ike," Clanton finally said.

"I ain't seen him." Brocius had never liked his whiny son. Ike was a worse coward than Billy Dale Spears. Ike stayed at the old man's ranch south of Tombstone and Brocius stayed away from him. He didn't like Ike's sense of humor or his ways.

"They accused him of stealing that horny thoroughbred stallion of Wyatt's. Sheriff Johnny Behan wouldn't serve the warrant. Hell, that damn horse was loose, running around on the desert, screwing every mare in Cochise County. Ike penned him up and was going to claim him when Wyatt rode down and raised hell. Shit, Earp should have kept the damn thing penned up. They've got a stray law in this territory."

"Ike was within his rights," Brocius agreed.

"Damn right he was. Them damn Republicans ain't nothing but trouble."

"It's all my fault."

"Aw, hell." The old man looked up at him across his

spoon of soup. "Hadn't been you, it would have been someone else."

"I guess." He was glad the old man wasn't still mad at him over the shooting. He'd never aimed to kill Charlie, and the man had told them so on his deathbed. But Brocius figured that lots of folks would go to their grave thinking he'd done it on purpose. A shame too because when Charlie was law, the gang members could get by with things at Tombstone. Not anymore.

"I'll send the men when you send the word." Then Clanton lifted the bowl of soup and slurped the rest down.

"Take care of yourself. See you," Brocius said as he stood up and started to leave. Clanton looked older to him than he could ever recall.

"Make sure we get that gold," the old man said, and belched loudly.

23

He climbed the porch steps of the hotel and glanced toward the noisy cantinas across the border in Mexico. The night was in full swing over there. He could see the light streaming out the front doors of the many establishments as a trumpet hit high notes and a guitar was strummed hard. Had she made it? He ran his palm up his smooth-shaven face. His shirt was freshly starched and pressed, as were his pants. He wondered if she would like to go eat. Over on the Mexican side there was a small cafe that served good food.

The clerk sent him to the second floor, Room 216. He climbed the steps and knocked on the thin paneled door.

"Yes?"

"Slocum," he said, looking up and down the empty hall lighted by small lamps in reflectors. The key in the lock clicked and she opened the door.

She was in a new split skirt and fancy vest, and she smiled at him. He nodded his approval.

"You hungry?" he asked.

"Yes."

"Good, let's go across to Ruby's cafe."

"Fine. I have wondered when you would come for me."

"Am I late?" he asked as she put on her shawl.

"No, but I was anxious to see you was all."

"Here I am. Was the stage ride down here all right?"

"Fine. The trip made me sick to my stomach like most stage rides do, but I've had time for it to settle."

"You all right now?"

"I am fine."

"Good. We leave Sunday morning for the desert."

"I will be ready."

They had a leisurely meal, and they both acted relaxed. The beans and rice, rich in cheese, and the goat meat roasted on mesquite proved tasty and tender. They both were full when the waitress brought them honey and sopaipillas.

"To our success," she said, and raised a half glass of wine toward him.

"Yes," he agreed, seeing something new in her blue eyes. A hazy look, perhaps too much wine, perhaps something new that had not shone there before.

"How do you live like this?" she finally asked.

"Don Alvares pays me well."

She nodded her head. "He must." Then, with a look of mischief, she swiped her index finger through the honey on her plate and held it to his mouth to let him lick it off like a candy stick.

They exchanged looks as he grasped her fingers, turned them, and finished off the last traces of the honey. Her face paled. Then she wet her lips until she finally looked away.

"I remember what you said." She swallowed hard. "I am trying to do that—go on with my life."

"No rush," he said, and released her fingers.

"A good thing," she said, sounding relieved, and her shoulders slumped.

Afterward he took her back to the hotel. They parted and he rode back to camp. In his bedroll away from the fire, his hands clasped under his head, he looked up at the Big Dipper and North Star. Mrs. McCoy was a very proper woman, still very married despite her husband's death, but infatuated with this search for the gold. He even felt a little twinge of hope that there would still be such a treasure when they got there.

Sunday morning, he took the bald-faced horse to the hotel as his column of wagons streamed by into Mexico. The bribed official waved each wagon and cart past with false papers and his own money envelope in his hand. Slocum went inside the hotel and found her standing in the lobby with her two bags and a bright smile.

"I was worried that you were going to leave me when I saw the wagons go by," she said, a flush of embarrassment on her cheeks.

"I'll pay the bill."

"No, I did already—with your money, of course." She looked so upset he wanted to hug her, but he decided to pick up her bags instead.

"I wouldn't have—"

"I know it was foolish, but I am a burden to you and I know how seriously you take your job of running the train."

He paused on the porch. The last wagon was clear of the border guard. Good. They were on their way. In ten days they would meet the ship in Libertad. He would be relieved—this was too late in the season to cross the dry land. Alvares had promised him there would be no more trains until the fall. Maybe the colonel's gold was buried in Libertad and the two of them would find it.

"Baldy is your horse," he said, and set down the bags. She gushed about the animal's good looks and raced down the stairs to pet his muzzle.

"He is gorgeous," she exclaimed.

"He ain't ugly, but he looks too much like something Crazy Horse would ride for me. Here, I'll help you up." He knew a woman would like such an animal.

"I've heard of Crazy Horse," she said, and swung up in the saddle. He handed her one bag, then took the other and mounted the bay. "Did you know him?"

"Casually. We'll put these bags in a wagon when we catch up," he said, and booted his horse after the train.

"Fine, lead the way."

The train snaked its way southward each day deeper into the organ-pipe forests, the lower elevation bringing more heat than the higher elevation of Nogales. They lost one ox to snakebite, and another died from heat exhaustion. Each day the temperature soared higher and higher. Slocum wondered if despite her broad-brimmed straw hat, Mrs. McCoy should ride in a wagon rather than on horseback.

Dust devils forty feet wide danced across the desert in funnels that stretched to the sky. Sometimes they ripped through the train, scattering sombreros and threatening to rip the men's clothes off their backs. Eyes filled with grit, the drivers would swear at the retreating columns as if they had come on purpose.

The only wind was too hot to enjoy. Like a furnace blast, it dried their eyes and breathed hot air at them. Heat waves rose, distorting even the shimmering lake mirages that floated before them offering the lure of cool water. In the midst of their strife with the weather, a cart's wheel broke and then shattered. Slocum realized it was beyond repair when he rode up and appraised the damage. He sent word for the train to circle around. Luckily the desert was flat and the vegetation limited to sparse greasewood, so they could manage a wide swing. Then he supervised the distribution of the sacked beans to other rigs as they came by. The oxen were unyoked and put behind the last wagon. The damaged cart was abandoned, and in a half hour the train was moving south again.

They reached Cienga. Sparse yellow leaves on the cottonwoods rattled like dry beans in a box in the hot wind. The scavengers had cleaned up the executed outlaws. Only a few scattered scraps of clothing and white bones remained, and traces of rope swung from the tree limb. Slocum was grateful for her sake that so little remained as he set up her tent with the aid of the man whose cart they'd abandoned.

"I wonder if I will have work after this," the man asked when they finished putting it up.

"You will have work. I will buy you a different cart in Libertad," Slocum reassured the man.

"Good, I have a large family to feed."

"There will be work, amigo." He clapped the man on the shoulder to reassure him.

"Even the marsh is drying up," she said, looking across the brown cattails and scrub willows.

"This land never forgets you," he said, and stretched his

arms over his head. "It's like a sidewinder waiting to strike when you least expect it."

"Is there enough water for the animals to drink and to fill our barrels?" she asked quietly. "I stopped by the tank. It looked very low."

"I saw it too. Perhaps in the morning we shall know if we can refill all our water barrels."

"No one lives out here?" She narrowed her eyes to the glare.

"There are many small ranches that survive at remote places like this one."

"What do they do for a living?"

"Raise some poor cattle, live off the desert."

"They must be very brave."

"They are, for they are at the mercy of outlaws and ruthless men."

"I know about that." She stepped over and hugged him hard. She nuzzled her face on his salt-stained shirt as if she wanted to be closer to him. He dared not touch her for fear she would flee.

"I'm sorry," she said, and straightened as if she regretted her actions. "The heat, the dust, and now the dry water hole—I am scared, but now I have you."

"You have me. This is not a good place for you either after all that happened."

"No, I have forgotten all that. I am doing as you said to do. I am trying to live my life for today."

"Eat some food and you will feel better. It will soon cool off when the sun sets."

"Don't worry about me. You have the train and all these men."

"We will all make it there together."

"I know—nothing, I'll be fine." She shooed him away.

He went to consult with Vasquez. He found the man busy stoking his fires and hanging iron pots on chains.

"Oh, we can make it," the older man reassured him. "I have gone two days on this road without water."

"We better ration it from here on."

"I will tell the older men. They can handle the others."

"Good." He wanted to be at Libertad and out of this hellhole. He raised his hat and mopped his gritty forehead with his kerchief. Three more days on the road. He wished he could sleep through it.

24

"The real gold train is coming," Julia whispered in his ear. Her excitement over the news seemed about to overcome her as she clung to him. Coming fully awake in the chair, he threw his arms around her as she climbed into his lap. How did she learn so much from that asshole clerk? She would make a great spy. He smothered her with kisses as he closed his eyes in relief. The gold would soon be his.

"When?" he asked as they huddled in the darkness of her casa. He could smell the odor of cigars and liquor that clung to her hair and clothing after she had worked all night in Rosa's cantina. He would take her away from this life when he had the gold. Maybe to San Francisco. He wanted to see such a large city, taste its luxuries. They would do that when he was rich.

"Next Thursday," she answered. "The decoy train will come through first to distract you." She fumbled with the buttons on his shirt.

"Then?"

"That night, the real one with the gold will come through at midnight. Are you not pleased?"

"Pleased? I am so excited. What is wrong?" he asked, blinking at her in the darkness.

"You forgot your fingers," she reminded him, and then she shoved his hand under her dress.

"Oh, yes."

155

"That's better," she said with a smile as his fingers teased her.

At first light Brocius rode down to the old man's place. He would need the men to meet him in the valley. If the gang members came through town, then the trains might be alerted. When he arrived at Clanton's and dismounted, the boy in charge of the horses came and took the reins. Brocius could see several of the men loitering around on the porch.

"What brings you out so damn early?" Vaught asked, leaning his shoulder against the porch post. He idly whittled on some cedar with a jackknife. There was something vacant about the man's sky-blue eyes. He had the cold look of a killer as he gazed to the north.

"Business with the old man," Brocius said, and brushed by him.

He located Clanton still seated at the long table inside spooning in some gruel. The Chinese cook was busily gathering dishes in a noisy clatter.

"You had breakfast?" Clanton asked Brocius.

"No."

"Lee, go get Brocius a big platter of food," the old man ordered, still holding his bowl in one hand, the spoon in the other. The Oriental left grumbling to himself about feeding cowboys all day long.

"Thanks," Brocius said, sitting down and looking around to be certain they were alone. "The gold's coming."

"I figured that's why you came." Clanton smiled; he rarely ever smiled, but some things made him grin, like the time they'd robbed this Mexican of five hundred dollars in gold.

"I will need the men to meet me at Cottonwood Spring Saturday morning. Tell them don't come up through Naco, stay away from there. It might tip our hand. My place to ambush the train is in the north end of the Penticellos at a spring where they will camp for the night. It is a perfect place. Four men could command it with rifles."

"What if they don't stop there?" Clanton held his spoon poised waiting for a reply.

"Then we will find them. But I am certain that they will."

"You're certain this train will have the gold?" Clanton raised his pale blue eyes and looked hard at him for a reply.

"There will be a decoy train first, then the one with the gold."

"I knew that day we broke you out of that Texas jail that someday you'd settle down and make a smart outlaw. I think this is going to be my payday."

"It is." Brocius settled back when the cook brought his heaping platter of eggs, meat, and biscuits and placed it before him. This robbery would be big.

Slocum rode beside Mrs. McCoy in the afternoon heat. He was gritty, with a sour body odor seeping from his clothing. He turned as one of the men shouted at his oxen. Had another animal collapsed from the temperature? He could hardly believe that they'd only lost three. But he knew that when you killed oxen, the situation was serious. They were like old shoe leather; they never wore out. They had changed mounts often to save their waning strength. The heat dulled men and their animals strayed from the road, causing delays as they tried to get back on track.

"How hot is it?" she asked.

"I imagine a hundred fifteen degrees. Maybe more today."

"Never will I complain about cold again. I can recall winters in Kansas when I longed for warm weather."

"Tell me about the treasure," he said to take her mind off the heat.

She looked around before continuing. "The strongbox is buried in the house's courtyard, ten steps north of the fountain."

"Sounds too easy."

"After all this time, I sometimes doubt it will still be there."

"It's worth a try," he said to encourage her.

"You are a hard man to defeat, Slocum."

The day dragged on, as did the next one, as they wound through the ovenlike canyons. In late evening, they

emerged from the mountains, and the first cool breeze from
the Gulf swept his face. He stopped his horse and pounded
his saddlehorn in gratitude for being there. The fishy odor
of the Gulf mixed with the desert's musk; they were close
to Libertad.

"I can smell it," she exclaimed, riding up beside him.

"Yes, we're almost there. In a few more hours we can
bathe in the sea."

"Good," she said. Then, as if she had been holding it
in, she burst out with: "What if someone lives in Talbot's
house?"

"We can cross that bridge when we get there."

"I just worried about it was all."

He booted his horse in close and squeezed her thin shoulders in a one-armed hug. She smiled back at his show of
affection. They moved on through the forest of towering
saguaros and great clumps of organ-pipe cactus.

Brocius started back to Julia's that afternoon. Only she and
the old man knew his business. He was very close to be-
coming a very wealthy man and he felt smug about it. Only
five days left to wait. He would have his black reshod. He
needed to buy a good rifle. There were many things he
would do. He had never had a home growing up; perhaps
he'd buy a ranch in Mexico like the old man's. Hire a
Chinese cook and a boy to stable his horse. She would like
that—Julia would like that.

How much of the bullion should he give her for all she
had done? Maybe enough for some new dresses. Anyway,
she could not spend that much money. Besides, she would
have the benefit of *his* money. He trotted the black for
home; his stomach upset with his expectations.

Thursday night Brocius was hidden from view, deep in the
dark shadows of a parked freight wagon and an empty
house. He sat in an old wicker chair so he could observe
the border crossing. Consumed with his eagerness, he
watched the second train file in under the starlight. The
plaintive husky honking of the mules and the dingle of the
lead mare's bell brought a smile to his face. He noted sev-

eral riders with drawn rifles who rode beside the train.

The first decoy train had passed in the light of morning, and must be a full day's travel ahead of this one. He had watched the guards search the ore. The rocks must have been sharp, for they'd often drawn their hands out as if cut. He'd watched the skinny clerk Phillipe come from the office, then talk to the train's leader, both nodding their heads. They thought their deception had worked.

Now he recognized the sombrero on a rider. The same young man wore it who oversaw the first pack train. He rode a swift gray horse of barb breeding. The animal looked like a pearl ghost as he swept up and down the line giving orders to the men.

In no time at all, the guards passed on the ore in the panniers. He heard one of the officals say aloud. "Ah, you bring some more glass to cut us. Why do you travel so late at night?"

"We are late. Trouble with the mules."

A good lie. Brocius rose. His bladder was so full he had to empty it. He stepped into the shadows and with great relief vented himself. Finished, he buttoned up his pants, considering going back to her place. She would be getting off work soon. He closed his eyes, hardly able to contain himself. In two more days, he would be a very rich man.

On Saturday morning, Brocius met the men at the lone cottonwood tree above the small spring that filled a small pool in a pocket of sand. They sat around on the ground smoking, and gave him a dull look when he arrived. He spotted the extra packhorses on the picket line with their mounts when he dismounted and dropped the reins. The black would ground-tie.

"What have you got?" Billy Dale asked, getting to his feet and brushing off the seat of his pants as he rose. "This whole damn thing is a secret between you and the old man."

Brocius looked them over: Billy Dale, Vaught, Stillwell Jack, Reno, Obregon, Begota, and a pimple-faced kid they called Shot. Seven men. The old man must have figured he made eight. Good enough.

"Gawdammit, you got us up here. What are we going to do?" Vaught demanded, grinding out his roll-your-own in the dirt beside his leg.

"At dark tonight we're going to ambush a gold train. You boys ready for some real gold?"

"How much?" Stillwell asked with a sneer on his upper lip.

"Listen, you ride for the old man like I do. You'll get your fair share."

"Yeah, like the stage robbery deal?"

"You want out?"

"No, but it better be good."

"It will be. Mount up. We've got to ride about twenty miles and get all ready for them."

They set out with him in the lead. Brocius was so excited inside that he could hardly contain himself. The best plan of his entire life, a chance to get rich, very rich, was only hours away. He checked the purple Chiricahuas to the west as they rode up the grassy flatlands. This would be his lucky day.

Disappointed, Slocum searched the placid blue sea. No ship had anchored yet; they must be early. The men were under orders to unyoke before they rushed off to the cantinas and whorehouse. He instructed the herder to take the stock north along the shoreline where there would be more grass as well as a spring of fresh water. His camp setup complete, he went and found Mrs. McCoy talking to Vasquez.

"It is not much of a port," she said, turning to Slocum and sounding disappointed.

"No, it is a poor place. Do you wish to walk the beach?" he offered. "The air is cool coming from the water."

"Yes, I do."

"Ah, señor, I will fix a meal for you and the señora in a few hours," the cook said.

"Fine," Slocum agreed, and the two of them started for the beach.

"Strange, there are no trees here," she said, gesturing to the vast stretch of rolling white sand.

"Perhaps a few palms in the village is all. Saltwater does not grow much."

"I guess not," she said as they struggled up the loose sand of a dune. He pulled her up to the top by the hand.

"Is there a place where I might go in the water?" she asked. She used her hand to shield her eyes from the water's glare.

"Do you swim?"

"Yes, some. Is it dangerous?" She frowned at him.

"No. We'll find a cove that is screened by the sand. Not many people out today."

"I may . . ." She turned away, obviously embarrassed.

"I won't stare at you."

"Good," she said, and they set out going north on the high mound that wound like a great serpent.

"This looks like a good place," he said, and they rushed down the slope to the lapping water.

She quickly sat on the sand and undid her button-up shoes. Then she checked on him as he sat beside her with his knees drawn up, and turned and removed her hose. In a flash, she was up and raised her split skirt so she could wade into the shallows.

"I hate to get my clothes wet," she said, looking undecided about how to go deeper.

"Take them off," he said.

"You don't think anyone will come?"

"No."

"Please don't stare." She tilted her head to the side for his answer.

"I won't."

"Then look away."

"Yes, ma'am." He turned on his butt, hugged his knees, and studied the blue cloudless sky. She was certainly modest for a married woman. Oh, well.

"You can look now!" she shouted.

He watched her paddling neck-deep in the soft sea. Her clothing was in a pile on the shore. A grin spread over his face. She was good in the water. A fresh breeze swept his face, and some of the stored heat of the past days evaporated from his skin.

• • •

Brocius had the horses picketed almost a half mile away up a side canyon so they would not answer the mules or put the pack train's men on guard. He put Stillwell and Reno on the north end where a trail led from the canyon. They were to cut off anyone's escape. He put the kid and Obregon on the west. Each man brought a rifle, ammo, and his blanket or ground cloth, so they could rest on it and be out of sight until the train arrived.

He sent Billy Dale and Vaught to the south end to hide and be the first force to strike when all of the train was by them. He and Begota would come down the sandy wash to complete the cross fire.

"No survivors are to be left," he told each one as he placed them.

A quail whistled in the brush, and a strong wind from the south threatened his hat. All was set. There were no tracks in the area of the springs. He had circled in from the north with the men and dispensed them wide of the valley floor and the spring. There was nothing to alert the train's guards.

He waited with his back to the eroded wall of the wash. The wind whistled above them. The Mexican Begota, seated close by with his rifle across his lap, smoked hand-twisted cigarettes one after another. Brocius wished for a drink of whiskey or anything strong. His skin was about to crawl. He waited and listened to the wrens flitting in a nearby mesquite tree.

He could hear the clack of hooves on the rocks upstream. Begota nodded that he too heard the animal's approach. A mule deer was coming down the wash. In silence, they waited and watched, wondering if the deer would show himself or slip away before he reached them. The velvet-horned buck soon came into sight, then, discovering the men, veered away and bounded up the far bank. He disappeared in a few high hops.

Brocius felt better. If a deer could not detect them until he was on them, they must be well concealed. He pushed his hat up and studied the sun. Mid-afternoon. They had hours to wait by his calculations. He hoped the others didn't get antsy on him and expose themselves.

The sun had dropped behind the Chiricahuas west of the valley. No pack train. A soft glow of twilight settled in the canyon. He knew the others must be getting tired of the long wait. Then Begota's eyes grew wider and he held up a finger. Yes, there—the sound of mules honking. They were coming. Both men pushed to their feet and worked the kinks out of their legs and limbs by walking around.

"We have waited a long time," Begota said, and checked his rifle chamber.

"Yes, but it will be worth it. Come, we must be closer when they begin to shoot."

The sound of rapid gunfire and the confusion of animals and men screaming filled the air as they rushed down the wash. A wide-eyed bucking mule almost ran over them. Brocius shot him in the face with his pistol. The mule went facedown in a pile.

"He may have gold on him, didn't want him to escape," he explained as they hurried on.

He fired his Colt at the outline of a rider shooting from horseback. The wounded man pitched off his mount. A packer on foot screaming in fear ran up the wash to escape. Brocius fired the Colt twice into the man's chest, and he collapsed to his knees hit hard and gripping himself. No time to waste another shot. Brocius rounded a mesquite tree as a dead man hanging over his saddlehorn pitched off his spooked mount.

More shots to the south, and then he saw the kid coming with his fists full of pistols and firing away at the guards. A rider charged around some brush to avoid the kid's bullets, and Brocius cut him down. Loaded mules and empty saddle horses ran about. More sporadic shots rang out all around. He whirled at the sound of something running, and barely avoided being run down by another crazed pack mule.

'You see any more live ones?" he shouted to Begota.

"They all look dead to me."

"Start catching mules!" he shouted to everyone. They

could not afford to lose one of them with their precious cargo.

He saw Billy Dale and Vaught coming, riding guard horses and leading several mules. Where was the leader of the guards?

"Did you see anyone on a gray horse?" he demanded.

'Yeah, we shot him, but he got away."

"Got away?" he demanded in disbelief. He'd meant to leave no witnesses.

"One damn Mexican can't do shit," Vaught said with a ring of impatience. "Besides, we hit him, he won't go far."

Something swirled in the pit of Brocius's stomach. They'd let the leader get away—how could they do that? He didn't care if a packer got away, but the train's leader had escaped. It wouldn't set well with the old man either.

"Look! Look!" Begota screamed, waving two gold bars at him. "We're all rich!"

"We got time for that later. I want every one of them bastards dead," Brocius shouted to them before gold fever overcame them. He took the bars from the man and put them back in the pack. "And I mean every last one."

"Cut their throats?" Vaught asked.

"Whatever. I just want to be sure they are all dead."

"You heard the man. Find them and be sure they're dead," the Texan said.

In the next few minutes, scattered shots were heard up and down the canyon, and the final gasps of victims with their throats sliced carried over the braying mules stomping around the bell mare that Brocius had found and hitched to a mesquite.

Vaught finally returned with a bloody knife in his fist. "They're all dead."

"Good. Gather the mules. Each man take a few head to lead back. Begota, you take Obregon and go put those packs from that dead mule up in the wash on one of our extra horses."

"How many dead men do you estimate?" Brocius asked Vaught as the twilight grew dimmer in the canyon.

"Two dozen, I figure."

"How many got away?"

The Texan shrugged. "Maybe that wounded one on the gray horse."

For a long while, Brocius considered the one who had escaped. If only there had been no witnesses. The notion that even one had gotten away niggled him. It was the leader of the guards too. Maybe he would die from his wounds.

Never mind. They were rich, and the old man would smile.

25

"Colonel Talbot's house burned down?" Mrs. McCoy whispered in disbelief.

"Shush, someone will hear us. Come on," Slocum said, taking her hand and leading her from the tent. Outside, he picked up his sack containing the lamp, rock pick, and small shovel. They carefully skirted around the men at the campfire singing songs and strumming their guitars under the starlight.

Once out of the men's hearing, and with the sounds of the surf pounding on the shore to cover their voices, he stopped so they could catch their breath.

"When did it burn down?" she asked.

"Several years ago, they say, and no one lives there now. It is down the beach a ways."

"But if it burned down, what is the use?"

"You said the gold was buried in the courtyard. It couldn't burn."

"Right. I just thought that there was no use if it was destroyed."

"Come on, we don't need to be discovered."

"Where did you learn all this?" she asked as they hurried up the broad sandy beach. The yellow lights of the village were on the rise to their left.

"From a man in a cantina. He knew the colonel. Said he was very much out of place down here."

166

"I can imagine. There is not even a plant besides those big cactus up in the desert. He came from the South."

"Magnolia trees and great oaks," he said, shifting his sack to the other shoulder. The memory was still bright for him of nights when the great tree canopies filtered the stars over his head.

"You obviously know about the South," she said.

"I was born there. This is very desolate compared to the Deep South."

He spotted the jagged walls of the ruins on the bluff, and they made their way there with some effort. He pulled her up in some of the tougher places, and halfway up the bluff they rested to catch their wind.

"I can see the ship out there." She pointed to the Gulf and the twinkling lights on the vessel.

"Captain Manard is anxious to get loaded and sail. He expects the weather to get rough with this wind and the clouds coming in from the Pacific Ocean."

"Does it ever rain in this country?" she asked.

"Sometimes it storms," he said, studying how to climb the rest of the face of the bluff. "Come on. I see a way to get up there."

"It's a long way down."

"Don't look down, look up." He tossed the sack up on the next ledge and took her hand in his. "Come on."

"You are a strange man, Slocum."

"Why?" he asked as they inched on their toes around the narrow outcropping. Over his shoulder, he could see the beach a hundred feet beneath them.

"You have never . . . I mean, well . . ."

"Watch your step. You mean, taken liberties with you?"

"Oh, oh," she said as if she was about to fall. He grasped her arm and pulled her onto the rock beside him.

"Yes," she gasped, and hugged the boulder. "Whew, that was close."

He leaned over and kissed her mouth. She clung defensively to the wall. Her eyes blinked in disbelief when he removed his lips from hers and then stayed close to her face.

"Did you mean something like that?"

"I didn't mean you had to now."

"Come on," he said. "There are some old stairs ahead carved in the rocks."

"Thank God," she said.

The house's broken walls stood out against the night sky when they reached the archway. He lighted a small candle in a reflector. It would be hard to see it from a distance and the flickering light would help them. Great charred roof and ceiling beams that had fallen in blocked their way beyond the open gateway. He raised the lamp and then lowered it looking to find a way in.

"Where would the courtyard be?" she asked, bumping into his back in an effort to stay close.

"Inside there somewhere, I suppose. We might be able to crawl under the beams and get in there."

Something scurried across the ground and she shrieked. "What was that?"

"A pack rat, I guess."

"A rat!"

"He won't hurt you. Now come on."

"Oh, I don't know why I'm doing this," she moaned. "I hate rats."

"You want to carry the light or drag the sack?" he asked.

"I'll take the sack, but don't you dare show me a rat."

On their hands and knees, they crawled and wiggled under the fallen timbers. The effort was slow, and at last he discovered they could go no further.

"It didn't work," he said flat on his belly.

"What didn't?"

"We have to go back and find another way."

"There better not be any rats back there."

He managed to slowly turn around, and spotted another small space with starlight beyond. His heartbeat quickened. "Wait. I think we can go this way."

"Good," she grunted from on her stomach.

"We can get out from under these beams anyway," he said, and pushed the lamp ahead. He slithered after it on the silt and ashes.

At last, on his hands and knees, he stared into the courtyard. Starlight shone on the tall fountain. He shook his head to be certain he wasn't dreaming.

"We've found it!" she said in a hushed voice, and clapped him on the shoulders. Then she squirmed over on her elbows and her mouth closed on his in a wild kiss. Hungry and twisting, she sought him until they both were out of breath. Side by side, they sat up on their knees and recovered.

"How far north of the fountain is it buried?" he asked.

"Ten paces."

Pushing off his knees, he rose to his feet with some effort, then pulled her up to her feet. He handed her the small lamp and then began to search the sky above the jagged wall for the Big Dipper. The sight of the seven stars drew a grin from him as he backed to the rim of the fountain's dry bowl and faced in the direction of the North Star. One, two—he counted until he planted his feet the tenth time.

"This the place?" he asked.

"I hope so."

He reached over and blew out the candle as he studied the tiled floor.

"Why do that?" she asked.

"So we don't attract anyone. I can see to dig. Who did the colonel give this information to?"

"One of Talbot's cousins in Texas. He lost the map to Roger, my husband, in a card game."

Slocum began whacking the tile with the hand pick to get under the edge. The mortar was hard after years of drying. But fleck by fleck, he soon had the first piece freed. He tossed it aside and it clattered across the floor as she knelt beside him anxious to see everything. Other tiles came easier, and soon he was digging looser fill out of the hole. A mound of dirt began to rise beside them as he used his muscles on the shovel to scoop it out and toss it aside.

"No word how deep it would be?" he asked.

"No," she said, biting a fingernail.

"It might not be here, you know."

"I know, but I'll feel like a fool if it isn't here. How deep are you now?"

"A foot, maybe eighteen inches." He set his hat aside

and used the hand pick to break loose some more dirt. Then the thud of something hollow made his heart stop.

"What was that?" she gasped, and tried to see in the hole as their shoulders rubbed together.

"I hit something in there besides rock and dirt," he said, using his hands to sweep away the sand and crumbling dirt.

"What is it?"

"Looks like the metal-bound edge of a strongbox."

Her fingers closed on the top of his shoulder and dug in his flesh. He wanted to warn her. The box could be empty. His heart began to pound and his temples hurt with the thud of a headache. He moved her aside and used the pick to dig some more. The job was slow and tedious. Inch by inch, he exposed more and more of the box.

"Oh, I'm so excited I can hardly stand it."

"So am I," he said, changing hands with the pick to dig away at the resistant soil.

"Don't look," she said with a sigh. "But I must go pee."

"No worry, go over there," he said as she rushed across the gritty courtyard. With newfound vigor, he continued picking and prying until at last, using the small spade for a fulcrum, he lifted out the heavy two-by-three strongbox and with some effort set it on the tile beside him. She rushed back and squatted down with her hands clasped together to view it.

"It has a lock," she said in disappointment.

"Had one," he said, and broke it open with the hammer end of the pick. The hasp fell apart and he undid it.

"Hand me the light," he said, fishing a match out of his vest with a trembling hand. He struck the lucifer on the side of the box and then lighted the lamp.

"I'm afraid to look," she said.

"What will you do if there is lots of money in it?" he asked, holding down the lid with the flat of his hand.

"I guess go back to Kansas."

"I thought you said you were going to live it up if you got rich." He frowned at her.

"Open it," she said, and tried to get by him to reach the lid.

"Wait. This money could change your life." He held her by the forearms to contain her. "What are you going to do if there is a fortune in here?"

"I had a long time to think on it while you were gone and all. I decided if there was enough money, I would go back to Kansas and I would buy a respectable hotel."

"How respectable?"

"Slocum! Very respectable."

"Good," he said, and released her arms. In her haste, she spilled over the top of him and threw back the hinged lid.

"My God, there's money in it!"

He held the lamp up as she sifted the golden coins from one hand to the other. A dull familiar glitter reflected off them, and he knew they were real and there were lots of them. The coins clanking together had the ringing sound of gold.

"There must be a million of them," she cried. Then she began to kiss him frantically. She poured coins by the handful down the front of his shirt and hugged his face to hers as they kissed. He closed his eyes and savored her attention. There must be at least a million!

26

"If you give these gold bars to them boys, why, they'll go flashing them around here and have the law down on all of us in ten minutes. We better ship it to a man I know in Denver. He can remelt it and then they can't trace it," the old man said. "Gold bullion ain't like gold coins or money. You can't spend it."

"You better tell the boys. They damn sure ain't going to be happy. They figured all the way back that they're pretty rich." Brocius shook his head in defeat.

"Be pretty dumb to go spend these bars here. The law would trace this gold by the stamp on it to the robbery, and we all could hang."

Hands behind his back, Brocius paced the tile floor. "How long will that take? To remelt it?"

"Couple months to ship it and him to do it and get it back. Why? You restless?"

"Gawdammit!" Brocius slammed his fist on the table and a few of the gleaming gold bars fell off the stacks. "I figured I was a rich sum-bitch when I got this damn gold. Now we've got to screw around with some bastard in Denver to remelt it. Hell, I wanted to go see the damned world, and I'm broke as shit here and have how much? Two hundred thousand dollars in gold here?"

"I can make you a loan."

"I don't want a damn loan." He slammed on his hat and

charged for the door. He paused and looked back. "You send that to him and get my money. Ain't no way left to make an honest living, is there?"

"Will you be up on the border if I need you?" the old man asked.

"Why, hell, yes. Ain't got any money to be anywhere else." He slammed the door and ignored all the questions of the others, who rose to their feet on the porch at his appearance.

"Don't ask me. Ask him!" he said, and stormed off to get his horse.

"You figured out who killed Perkins and that kid?" Vaught asked. His shoulder leaned against the corral post when Brocius led the black out to saddle him. The Texan whittled away.

"Wasn't you, huh?" Brocius tossed on the pads and then slung on his rig.

"Nope. Only leaves one sum-bitch then, don't it."

"He had a reata on his saddle when I checked it that night."

"Switched it when he got here," Vaught said, and cut a curl out of the red block in his hand. "He had Perkins's hemp on his horn coming home."

"You knowed that all this time and never said a word?" Brocius looked toward the porch. He could see Billy Dale up there talking to the others.

"I figured you'd figure it out by now. He likes them little boys."

"He won't long." Brocius mounted the black and reached in his saddlebag for the small piece of reata from the dead man's neck. He headed the black for the house.

"Billy Dale, get out here," he said, reining up short of the porch.

The cowboy blinked, stepping out into the bright sun, and tried to look up at him. "Yeah? What's wrong now?"

"You killed those little boys, didn't you?" Brocius demanded.

"What you talking about?" Billy started backing up, and the others scattered.

"You killed Perkins too. The reata that you hung him

with was a four-plait, and the one you replaced on your saddle when you got back was a three.'' He held the short piece out in his left hand.

''You know so damn much, you fat son of a bitch! You need to die too!'' Billy Dale growled in black-faced rage. He went for his gun.

Too late. He'd never more than cleared leather when the smoking Colt in Brocius's hand leveled three shots into his chest like thudding rocks on a pumpkin. They slammed him back against the porch post and he slid down it to his butt. His pistol fell on the ground.

''What the hell you done now?'' the old man shouted as he charged out the doorway.

''He's the one that killed Perkins and them two little boys.''

Clanton looked at the dying cowboy and then at the others, who nodded woodenly at him. He shook his head in disbelief and then went back inside.

When he arrived back at Naco, Brocius brooded all day at Rosa's. He drank too much while Julia slept. Finally he went back to her jacale and awoke her.

''Oh, Brocius.'' She sat up and hugged him.

''The damn gold ain't no good,'' he mumbled in defeat.

''You got it?'' Her eyes rounded in shock.

''Yeah, but we can't spend it. They will know that we stole it. It has a brand on it like cattle have. He has to ship it to Denver and melt it down, and then maybe we can cash it in.''

''He? Who is he? The old man?''

''Yeah. He's right too. Who would take gold bars for money? They would say, ah, this gold comes from the robbery.''

She nodded her head in grim realization. ''So when will it be back?''

''It may take months,'' he said.

''Poor baby, but you can wait.'' She gathered the sheet around her. Someone was coming. Brocius turned as the young girl Ramona, who washed dishes in the cantina, came to the open door.

"What is wrong, little one?" Julia asked.

"Many men come and ask about Curly Bill at the cantina."

"Who are they?" he asked, on his feet, Colt in hand.

"One man has his arm in a sling. They call him Tomas."

"Were they Mexicans or gringos with him?"

"Mexicans, but señor, they are very tough hombres. Rosa told them you were at the Clanton ranch."

"Did they ride there?"

"Yes. There were more men outside on horses too."

"Did this Tomas ride a gray horse?"

"*Sí.*"

"Why?" Julia asked.

He shook his head and stared out the door at the desert. They had let him get away.

The ship was hurriedly loaded and set to sail. Slocum watched the clouds draw up like a great snowy wall in the south. He watched the nervous captain, his cargo on board, lift anchor and sail from the harbor, anxious about the weather slipping up on them. Slocum had taken a bath and shaved, ready for the return trip. He searched the camp for Mrs. McCoy.

He found her down by the shore buying fish from some village fishermen for Vasquez. The fishermen carried the catch for her and she led them up the beach.

"We are eating fish tonight in camp," she said with a smile. "The señor and his sons have caught many today and sold them to me for ten pesos."

"Robbery," he said in English, displeased at her extravagant expenditure. Why, he could have bought them much cheaper.

"Oh, Slocum, it is nice to help these poor people." She swung on his arm to humor him.

"Take them to the camp," he said to the three men. Then he frowned as another notion struck him. "Wait. Tell me about the storm that comes. How high will the waves reach?"

"To the village," the man said, and waved his hands across the broad beach to the adobe hovels on the bluff.

"Thanks." he said, stunned by the knowledge as the wind stiffened.

"What is wrong?" she asked.

"If we don't get all these goods and wagons up there in the desert past the town, we may lose them when that storm down there strikes here. They'll get washed away."

"Oh, no. What can I do?"

"Ride up the beach to the herder and have him bring back the oxen as quick as he can. I'll send Vasquez to get the men and hire some more from the village to help us load up." His legs felt weighted with lead as he hurried to find the cook.

"What is wrong?" the fisherman asked in dismay, hurrying beside him. "The señora, she no wants the fish?"

"Yes, she does. She also wants to hire you for many pesos to load all these goods into the wagons and then help us get them up off this beach before the storm comes in."

"We can do that," the wrinkled fisherman agreed.

"We would be glad for the work," his boys agreed.

"Good. You start packing these boxes in that cart." He watched the rising wind sweep her skirt as she ran for her horse. Mounted, she whipped the pony with the reins until she disappeared over the dune as he explained to Vasquez about getting the men from town and hiring any other help he could. Already some of the drivers were coming down the swirling dunes from the village. They too knew something was wrong.

The wind had shifted. They had little time. Damn, he had forgotten about the storms and how they whipped up the Gulf. That was why the village was on that high bluff. They had to hurry. Each minute the waves were crashing like thunder higher on the beach. As the men arrived, he sent them to load. By hand, they dragged carts and wagons around to get them close to the piles of crates and goods brought from the ship. Vasquez returned with a couple dozen extra men and boys. They joined the others in the rush to load up.

At last the herd of oxen came in view. She and the boy were riding hard to get them to move into the gale. The wind swept his hat away. He recovered it and threw it in the cook wagon. No time for a hat. Big drops of rain began to pelt them as the day grew darker.

She had taken the tent down. It threatened to blow her and the shelter away. He grabbed it, and together they hurled it inside the back of the cook wagon, under the slapping tarp on the bows, to save it.

"Get your horse and ride!" he shouted.

"No! I can help!"

"Get your horse and ride now! I want you on high ground!"

A twelve-foot wave shot over them. When it passed, dripping wet, he shoved her toward the horse. Men were hitching oxen, cursing and shouting. Then they began to move out. At last all the rigs were hitched and moving; he headed down the beach to hurry the laggers. A bolt of lightning crashed and the boom of thunder deafened him. Rain blinded him as he waded into the rushing seawater to help them drive their teams. He looked back in time to see a great wall of water threatening him.

The twelve-foot wall flattened him. Then the undertow threatened to carry him back to the Gulf as he fought the fishy salt water. Below the surf, his boots became full of water, his clothing heavier, and he fought harder, swimming furiously until he crossed the top of the wave and was deposited in the shallows. Scrambling to his feet, he could see nothing in the dim light and hard rain. All his wagons had to be a hundred yards away. He slugged his way as fast as his wet weighted boots would carry him, listening to the wall building behind him and threatening him again.

Then, in a flash of lightning, he saw a rider coming on a horse. He hoped it wasn't her. She had no business there.

"Get on, señor," the herder boy shouted, and Slocum wasted no time swinging up behind the youth. The pony left in a jolt and strove hard to escape as the next wash of waves struck at the horse's heels. The flush of foamy water swept beyond them. Slocum would have never managed to run away from it on foot. They soon climbed the hill, and the boy stopped the pony among the wagons straining up the steeper sand dunes.

"Thanks," Slocum shouted to the boy.

"Your horse!" Vasquez cupped his hands to his mouth to talk over the rain and wind whipping them. He handed Slocum the reins. "Every wagon is up here."

"Good! They did wonderful! Mrs. McCoy? Have you seen her?" he shouted at the man. Where was she? He hadn't seen her in hours.

"In my wagon dry." Vasquez grinned. "That was very close. I too had forgotten the fury of the sea."

"We both did. Thanks," he said, mounting the bay pony and turning his head from the hard rain. His men had acted superbly. He had to thank them and also pay the villagers who'd helped him. He looked back in the darkness and saw the great swells and crashing surf piling over what had once been their beach.

"You all right?" he shouted at the back of the cook wagon. Her face appeared in the oval hole of the canvas tarp.

"I'm fine, but you need to dry out or you'll catch a cold."

"I need to get this wagon train in camp. Then I can do that," he said to put her off.

He waved to her as he rode out. There were many things to do. They had to get camped on high ground. The dry washes would soon be as dangerously flooded as the beaches. More hard rain swept over him, chilling him to the skin as he rode by and encouraged the drivers. They were lined out and going up the road. They could camp at the base of the mountains for the night.

At last, with everything settled for the evening, he stripped off his wet shirt in her tent, then unbuttoned the top half of his underwear and took it down. She dried his back with a Turkish towel. The rain had moved away, and cool air filled the land as twilight settled on the pristine desert.

"I counted the money this morning," she said, pausing in her work.

"How much is there?"

"Three thousand, four hundred, and thirty-two dollars."

"No millions?"

"No, but a lot of money, though."

"Is it enough to buy a respectable hotel in Kansas?"

"All of it would. But half of it is yours." She looked at him with a frown.

"I've never owned half a respectable hotel in Kansas before."

"Are you serious?" She squinted at him in disbelief.

"Never more so. Why, I could come by and check on you."

She shook her head as if he was impossible. "Stand up and take off those wet clothes. You're only half dry."

"You serious?"

"Never more so. I could check on *you*."

He rose from the folding chair, undid his clammy wet pants, and fought them off. Then, with a shrug, he stripped off his underwear and stood naked for her. She started to dry him with the towel.

"Oh, my God," she said, and buried her face in his chest as if to hide her eyes. "You certainly are—large."

"Your man wasn't this large?" He saw the redness rising in her face when he looked down at her.

"Roger? Heavens, no, not half this large." Then she turned her face up for him to kiss her. He clutched her to him. They were going to celebrate their hotel partnership. That is, if he could get in the front door.

Brocius was dead drunk. When he returned to her place late that night, he felt nothing. Numbly, he dismounted. He never undid his girth or unsaddled his horse, simply staggered up on the porch.

"Is that you, my baby?" she called out.

"Yeah. Them bastards killed the old man and everyone else tonight—no one survived. They burned the damn ranch house down. It blew up with some kinda bomb or dynamite. All my gold is gone. All my hard work, everything, it is all gone." He staggered into the house and she caught him. Too dizzy to stand, he teetered on his boot heels. The old man was dead. Everyone was dead.

"Someone is coming. I hear horses," she said, and shoved him. In his drunken stupor, he fell out the open window onto the ground, and sprawled underneath the broken-down wagon parked there. Rifle shots shattered the night's silence like a Gatling gun. The air became alive with whining bullets, red-streaking muzzles, and the acrid smell of gun smoke. Unable to rise up, he heard her screams of pain as more shots followed, and then all was quiet. His fingers closed on a fresh wad of chicken manure, and he squeezed it with all his might.

"The *puta* was in there with him," someone complained in Spanish. Their horses snorted, stomped, and milled in front and on the other side of the jacale. The broken-down wagon concealed him.

"She shouldn't have hid him out is all I can say. Let's go."

Damn bastards. They'd killed his sweet Julia too.

"The desert is already greening up," Mrs. McCoy said to Slocum as they rode together on the road a good distance in front of the train. He smiled at her. The daytime heat had been tempered by the afternoon thunderstorms. Water was no problem, and the trip back had been uneventful.

"We'll be in Nogales tonight," he said.

"Can we stay together in a hotel room?" she asked, looking ahead as if she dared not turn and face him.

"Oh, perhaps, but I like sleeping on the ground."

"Well, I'd like a real bed for one night. Who's coming?" she asked.

"Looks like a buckboard and a rider." He frowned. At the distance he recognized Tomas's hat, but a woman was driving the team. The rider on the gray horse was Don Alvares. What was wrong?

Juanita planted her button-up shoes on the dash and in a flash of white petticoats, she hauled the team to a stop. Tomas grinned, holding the back of the spring seat with his left hand, his right arm in a sling.

"Don Alvares, what's wrong?" Slocum asked, looking them over with a wary eye.

"Good day," Alvares said to Mrs. McCoy, and took off his hat.

"Mrs. McCoy," Slocum said to introduce her. "Don Alvares."

"It is my pleasure, dear lady."

"Why are you all out here?" Slocum asked.

"First, those bounty hunters are waiting for you in Nogales," Alvares said. "The Abbott brothers. So you can't go there. Secondly, the cowboys led by Curly Bill attacked the pack train and stole the gold bars."

"He was shot?" Slocum pointed to Tomas and frowned with concern.

"Yes, but my son-in-law Tomas and others revenged the deaths of his poor comrades. Old Man Clanton and the cowboys are dead. They think they got Curly Bill too."

"Who has the gold?" Slocum asked.

"We couldn't find it. But there is more in the mines," Alvares said. "You, my friend, should take this good horse."

"I hear you, sir." He rode over and smiled at the pair in the buckboard. "Do I get to kiss the bride?"

"Certainly," Tomas said proudly with a grin. Juanita leaped up and kissed him hard as he leaned out of the saddle.

"Take care of that boy, he's a keeper," he said to her, and winked at her as he reined his pony around "Don Alvares, I can't take that good gray horse of yours. Why, folks would recognize him anywhere. Let me talk to Mrs. McCoy in private for a minute, and then I'll collect my wages and ride. I sure appreciate you all coming out here to warn me."

"Those brothers came to the ranch looking for you and I ran them off," Juanita said.

Tomas nodded. "She did it with a shotgun," he boasted.

"I can believe that. Excuse me." Slocum rode over to Mrs. McCoy, and she fell in beside him with her bald-faced horse. They trotted up on the hill as the creak of the train's carts and the roll of iron wheels became louder.

"Sorry, but I have to leave," Slocum said.

She nodded slightly. "I think I know why."

"What town's my hotel going to be in?"

"How about Hayes?"

"Good town. Keep the porch light on and things respectable. I'll be by to see how we're doing from time to time."

"You know, Slocum, I think you *will* drop in."

"I *will* come by one day." He leaned over and kissed her. Then he straightened. "Good luck, partner."

"Thanks for everything, Slocum. You be careful."

"I will." He smiled at her, and then he rode over to where Alvares sat the gray horse.

"I wish I could do something else for you," Alvares said. He held out a wallet to him and Slocum thanked him. He stuck it inside his shirt without looking at it. He trusted the man's generosity.

"She says she is going to have my grandson." Alvares motioned to his daughter Juanita and Tomas in the buckboard talking to Mrs. McCoy.

"Be a fine one."

"Maybe some day he could even replace you."

"No, he'll be better than that. You tell the men that they were good workers and my trusted friends."

"I will. God be with you, my friend."

Slocum nodded, and waved to Mrs. McCoy and then Tomas and Juanita.

Then he spurred the bay horse into a short lope to the east. His plan was to make a long swing around Nogales. Somewhere up on Patagonia Creek, there was a Mexican woman called Ruby who would board him for the night. She could probably trade the bay for a fresh horse, no questions asked.

In the distance, the Huachuca Mountains rose like a great purple bowl turned upside down. He should have let Tomas taken the wagon train while *he* guarded the gold pack train. Too late now. He leaned back as the bay charged down the hillside. He would need to make distance between him and the Abbotts.

Epilogue

Slocum easily evaded the Abbott brothers in Arizona that summer, and pushed his way over into New Mexico. Ten years later Slocum was dealing blackjack in Ned Turner's Saloon in Trinidad, Colorado, when he read the news in the *Denver Republican*. In an interview, Doc Holliday told how Deputy U.S. Marshal Wyatt Earp had killed the legendary Curly Bill Brocius in a shoot-out with some stage robbers near the Whetstone Mountains southwest of Tombstone. But two years after that, Slocum saw Brocius or his double in Fort Laramie, Wyoming, with a cattle outfit.

Then there were rumors that the Texas Rangers had shot Curly Bill in a roundup of rustlers near El Paso. The truth of the matter was Curly Bill Brocius didn't quit breathing until 1918. While working on Christmas Day in his livery stables in Free Liberty, Texas, he was kicked by a mule in the chest, which broke six ribs and punctured his lungs. Pneumonia set in and he died three days later. His tombstone in the Free Liberty Baptist Cemetery read "William Brocius." He never used the handle "Curly Bill" after his Arizona days. The marker is gone now, but his bones, or what's left of them, are planted in the Lone Star State.

The site of the pack train robbery became known thereafter as Skeleton Canyon, and a decade later, Geronimo sat at the very same place and surrendered to General Miles.